GLADIATOR ISLAND

ISLAND

The Arrival
COREY O'NEILL

E

EPIC
Press

The Arrival
Gladiator Island: Book #1

Written by Corey O'Neill

Copyright © 2017 by Abdo Consulting Group, Inc.

Published by EPIC Press™
PO Box 398166
Minneapolis, MN 55439

Cover design by Laura Mitchell
Images for cover art obtained from iStockPhoto.com
Edited by Leah Jenness

LIBRARY OF CONGRESS CATALOGING-IN-PUBLICATION DATA

Names: O'Neill, Corey, author.
Title: The arrival / by Corey O'Neill.
Description: Minneapolis, MN : EPIC Press, [2017] | Series: Gladiator Island ; book #1
Summary: Troubled teen Reed Mackenzie embarks on Ship Out, a three-month rehab program
on a boat that sails around the world. When the kids are taken to a mysterious island against
their will, things take a sinister turn, and Reed wonders if the strange place is part of the Ship
Out program at all.
Identifiers: LCCN 2015959397 | ISBN 9781680762679 (lib. bdg.) |
ISBN 9781680762884 (ebook)
Subjects: LCSH: Adventure and adventurers—Fiction. | Interpersonal relationships—Fiction. |
Survival—Fiction. | Human behavior—Fiction. | Young adult fiction.
Classification: DDC [Fic]—dc23
LC record available at http://lccn.loc.gov/2015959397

EPICPRESS.COM

For Josh,
for your love and guidance

CHAPTER 1

The Ship Out program was going to change me. At least, that's what my dad promised. Or threatened, depending on how you look at it.

On the long drive, my mom kept trying to hand me the thick blue folder she got when signing me up for Ship Out. On the front, there was a picture of smiling kids waving from the deck of a sailboat. Across the bottom it said: *The ocean is the best setting in the world for an individual to grow and heal.*

That statement was ridiculous. I thought of at least three better places to do all of those things, which I quickly pointed out.

"School," I called up to the front seat.

"Hiking on a mountain."

"And, Dad . . . what about yoga class?" I suggested. I was being a smartass, and I craned to catch my dad's tight-lipped frown in the rearview mirror. I couldn't help but enjoy trying to get a rise out of him. I could tell that if I pushed him a little more—just told another dumb joke, even—he'd probably start exhaling loudly through his mouth, a deep breathing technique he did when he was especially pissed.

"Reed. Just look at the packet, okay?" my mom said, her voice strained. Typically a bottomless well of patience, I could tell she was also fed up.

We'd been driving all morning and every inch of me ached from the monotony and boredom of being trapped in a small car for hours on end. I had no tablet, no wristlet, no music, and no friends to break up the time.

Finally, I took the folder from my mom. She couldn't help but smirk when she handed it back.

"Really? Score one for me," she joked and pumped her fist, trying to get me to smile.

The kids on the cover of the folder were all good-looking and healthy, a sun-kissed cross-section of America's teenagers. None looked mental, or like druggies or criminals. No delinquents in the bunch. The picture wanted me to believe they were happy. Obviously the sea had helped them *grow and heal.*

The Premier Solution in Oceanic Therapy, the folder said in big white letters. Although I'd never heard of Ship Out before, I had a good idea what kind of program it was. A guy I knew from school, Jeremy, was taken to a forest last summer to kick his drug habit as part of some crazy, scared straight rehab deal. I heard that he was dropped alone in the middle of the California wilderness with nothing more than the camping supplies he could carry on his back—a tent, some dried food, a compass, and that's about it. He was forced to stay out there for six weeks all by himself, without speaking to anyone that whole time.

To me, this 'oceanic therapy' thing sounded like a pretty sweet setup for the parents, like a summer vacation from a kid who didn't live up to expectations. I opened the folder and a close-up of a cute girl with windswept hair smiled back at me. The sun beamed down on her, and the sea was at her back. At the bottom, there was a photograph of a psychiatrist named Dr. Wingett, the creator of Ship Out.

WE SUPPORT YOUR AT-RISK TEEN THROUGH REVOLUTIONARY OCEANIC THERAPY METHODS

At Ship Out, we know dealing with a troubled teenager is challenging and scary. We're here to help and guide you.

Ship Out was created to provide confidential treatment to at-risk teens and their families. With the industry's most clinically sophisticated oceanic therapy methods and experienced practitioners, Ship Out was founded on the principle that troubled teens and their families should be dealt with firmly, but with compassion.

I pressed my forehead into the window and sighed loudly enough for my parents to hear. I'd been in and out of various therapy programs for the past two years, so this all sounded familiar, but on a sailboat—for three months. I paged through the rest of the folder. It was filled with big promises splashed across photographs of kids working hard on a boat's deck—*Lifetime friendships. Adventure. Soul discovery.*

My mom turned back in her seat, looking at me hopefully. "It almost sounds fun, right?"

"Ha, yeah, like a dream come true. Well, at least I'll come back with an awesome tan."

My dad glared at me in the mirror, and my mom reached back and squeezed my hand.

I pulled it away and slouched back in the car seat. As I stared out the window, the midday sun warmed my skin and soon I was sleepy. I decided that the only thing left to do was nap. I closed my eyes and started to doze off, hoping that when I woke up, maybe my parents would've changed their minds and we'd be heading back home.

I awoke when the car slowed and then came to a stop. I opened my eyes, and ahead at the end of the road, I saw a long, white sailboat standing tall above the water.

"Hallelujah, we've arrived," my dad declared, stretching his arms up and out against the tan ceiling of the car. He put on his baseball cap and sunglasses, his go-to "disguise" when he didn't want people to immediately recognize him.

"You think that really works, huh?" I asked him, and my mom shot me a look.

Next to the boat, on the dock, a group of about thirty people huddled loosely around a tall, overly tanned man who was speaking to them. He stopped abruptly when he saw us pull up, and hustled toward us.

When we got out of the car, he was standing right there, smiling widely with large, perfect teeth. "You must be the Mackenzie family. You're the last to arrive!"

My mom glanced down at her watch and apologized. "Oh I'm sorry, I thought we were supposed to be here at two."

"That's right," the man said, looking at us and continuing to smile broadly. There was a moment of awkward silence. It seemed like this would be the right time for the guy to introduce himself. Instead, my dad chimed in.

"Tim Mackenzie. Nice to meet you," he said, sticking out his hand.

"Oh, I know who you are. Of course. Big fan, actually. My name is Titus, and it's my pleasure, believe me. Rachel, good to meet you," he said to my mom. He then reached over and gripped my shoulder. I stood more upright, not wanting him to sense me wincing under his grasp.

"I'll take care of your boy. Don't you worry about a thing," Titus said while smiling at my mom. Her face softened as Titus looked at her.

He then turned his gaze toward me. "Reed McKenzie, we've got big plans for you."

It struck me as a weird thing to say and I wasn't sure how to respond. I stared back at him blankly.

My dad interjected, "Please don't treat Reed any—"

Titus quickly stopped him. "Oh, Tim. We'd never tolerate preferential treatment, if that's where you're headed."

"Yes. Exactly. Good," my dad said, pleased.

"Now, let me go introduce you to everyone else," Titus said. He reached to grab my duffle and suitcase from me. I pulled them away, insistent on carrying them myself.

"Good boy," he responded, grinning at me, before leading us toward the group.

I distrusted Titus immediately. His perma-smile and lingering eye contact felt like acts of aggression instead of friendliness. But I could tell my parents liked him.

"Told you he'd be in good hands . . . if Jorge says something is the best, it's the best," I overheard my dad say to my mom. Jorge had been my dad's spiritual guide for the past ten years. I couldn't stand the guy and his new age crap that my dad regurgitated. My dad always thought Jorge was right, so it went without saying that he believed this plan to send me to Ship Out was brilliant.

I couldn't make out the rest of my parents' conversation, but I turned back and my mom smiled at me, obviously relieved.

As we approached the dock, a small tan girl with auburn hair piled on top of her head waved at me. She was sitting cross-legged on her suitcase. Grumpy-looking people I assumed were her parents stood behind her, frowning with arms crossed tightly over their chests. I glanced to the side and behind me, and then waved back, trying to look confident. My parents came up beside me as we joined the group.

"Everyone, this is Reed. He's the last Ship Out mate we've been waiting on," Titus said, slapping me across the back. I quickly scanned the group. There were only eight kids in total, including me. A dark, good-looking guy with shaggy black hair pushed back from his face with a stretchy headband nodded my way and the others stared at me blankly, or didn't look my direction at all. "Please put your luggage over there," Titus instructed, pointing to a fence next to the boat.

"We'll be going through each one to screen for contraband . . . phones, drugs—recreational, of course—candy, video games . . . basically, anything fun is not allowed. Sorry." Titus said. "In fact, if we find any of that, we'll just keep it for ourselves," he joked, smiling widely and chuckling. I took this as an attempt at being funny when the two other

Ship Out staff members standing behind Titus also laughed, nodding in agreement. The parents of the group smiled, being polite.

I carried my suitcase and duffle bag to the fence and dropped them with a sigh. This sucked—I hated this Titus guy already. As I was standing there looking out at the ocean, I felt someone staring at me and turned around.

"Hey there," the small girl with red hair said, standing just a foot away, looking up at me with squinty green eyes. "Aww. Don't cry. It's only three months."

Did I seem that miserable? I forced myself to perk up and appear calm and nonchalant, something I had become good at faking the last couple of years.

"Nah, I'm all good. I'm just sad it's *only* going to be three months, actually," I joked, and she laughed. I reached out my hand. "I'm Reed, nice to meet you," I said.

"I know . . . I mean, Titus already introduced you. I'm Delphine."

We sat there for a moment staring at each other. I was unsure what to say next.

"So, whatchya in for?" she finally asked.

"Wouldn't you like to know?" I responded, not really interested in sharing my baggage with someone I just met.

"Well, suit yourself. But, Reed Mackenzie, I'll tell you one thing," she said, looking at me with her pale green eyes.

"Yeah?" I asked.

"I can just tell that we are going to be friends."

"Yeah, I think you might be right . . . " Before I finished talking, she was already skipping ahead to an awkward-looking guy walking with his head down, a brown mop of hair obstructing his eyes. "Hi there! I'm Delphine!"

"Dude," a voice behind me suddenly chimed in. I glanced over, and the tall guy with the headband was now striding alongside me. "She's a cutie, huh?"

Caught off-guard, I fumbled a response. "What? Oh, her?" I asked, nodding in Delphine's direction. "I guess. She's kind of strange though," I said.

"Ha. You trying to throw me off? It's okay, just keep on playing cool. But, I'm guessing we may just have to fight for her," he joked, nudging me in the arm. Delphine glanced back at us and smiled and I was pretty sure she knew what we were talking about. She seemed very assured and forward, and different from any girl I'd ever met. I couldn't put my finger on it.

"Shh . . . dude! She can hear us!" I muttered to him, feeling embarrassed. He just grinned back at me.

"I'm Micah. Nice to make your acquaintance. If this is the last chance for us fuckups, it's not too shabby, right?" he asked, nodding toward the boat. I saw the name painted on the side was *The Last Chance*.

Dr. Wingett must have a twisted sense of humor.

"Yeah. Not too bad," I said.

We walked slowly. I wasn't eager to return to my parents, who were huddled in the larger group, waiting to say goodbye. My dad was hanging back and I caught him looking at his tablet. When my mom saw me returning, she nudged him sharply in the side and he rolled it back up and slipped it in his pocket.

When we got back to the group, Titus walked over.

"Okay guys, time to get moving. The sun is shining and the wind is at our backs. This moment is all we have, and it's perfect," he said. He turned his face toward the sky, outstretched his arms as if giving the sun a giant hug, and closed his eyes, exhaling loudly.

I couldn't help but laugh out loud and Micah smirked at me.

"Now, all together, let's take a deep breath and

shut our eyes, and each do our part to envision calm waters and forward progress," Titus proclaimed. And to my surprise, nearly all the adults followed his direction, turning their heads downward, as if in church. I didn't want to listen, but I bent my head when my mom poked me sharply in the side.

We stood there in silence for what felt like forever, hearing nothing but the sound of the small waves lapping against the boats tied up in the marina.

"Okay, that was nice, right?" Titus asked. He looked around at the group. I caught Delphine's attention for just a moment, and she rolled her eyes at me.

Suddenly, Titus got very serious-looking and declared, "Well, I'm afraid it's time to say your goodbyes, everyone. And make them count. As you may or may not know, we advocate conscious separation so our contact back to the 'real world' will be non-existent once we depart," Titus said.

"Unless, of course, we run into any problems, which never happens," he continued. "It's actually a good thing if you *don't* hear from us!"

The two crew members behind him nodded.

I turned to my mom and dad. My mom's frown lines furrowed and the threat of tears glinted in her eyes. I'd seen this expression many times before. I knew she was thinking about my brother, and about me, but mostly about James and what happened. I couldn't believe she was sending me away.

"You're really going to do this?" I asked her in one last-ditch effort to salvage my summer.

"We've made up our minds, Reed. This program comes very highly recommended by Jorge, and you're lucky you even got a spot," my dad said. He was not one to negotiate. "And your mom is on the same page."

"Yes. I am. You're doing this, Reed. No sense in trying to change my mind," she replied.

"But I'm going to be seasick," I said. "And, what about wrestling camp?"

I made the decision months ago that I wouldn't be wrestling anymore, but I was pulling out all last-ditch stops to reverse the course of the next three months. My days of spending every waking hour training were over—my two state championship cups meant a whole lot more to my parents than they did to me. These days, all of my trophies sat up high gathering dust on a shelf in my room. I used the golden cups to hide weed, which always got a good laugh out of my friends.

Instead of being stuck in a stinky gym all day, I was supposed to be partying all summer—camping, at pool parties, and celebrating the end of my sophomore year—and I was going to miss out on it all.

My dad put his arm firmly around Mom, like he was reminding her that what was done was done and that they were a united front.

"Just think of this as an once-in-a-lifetime adventure," he said, pulling me in for a tight, long embrace. I couldn't remember the last time he hugged me when it wasn't just for show in front of others. I looked around to see who was watching. Sure enough, Titus was standing on the boat deck, smiling down in our direction, nodding in approval.

"It's time to grow up, Reed," my dad couldn't help but say, and I pulled away. My dad didn't know anything about me these days. My mom wiped away at her runny nose and reached over to squeeze my arms, looking me in the eyes.

"You're going to be okay," she said. I couldn't tell if she was trying to reassure herself or me. She grabbed me for a hug and I wriggled free, not wanting to give her the satisfaction.

"Thanks a lot, guys," I spat out and spun around, facing the boat. I started up the ramp. As soon as I began walking away, I felt a twinge of regret for not hugging my mom back.

When I turned back one last time, the sun blinded my eyes and all I could see was my parents' silhouettes, waving as I walked away from them.

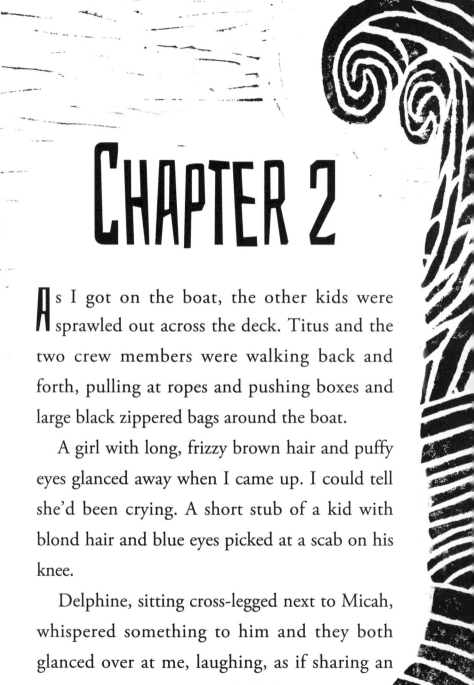

CHAPTER 2

As I got on the boat, the other kids were sprawled out across the deck. Titus and the two crew members were walking back and forth, pulling at ropes and pushing boxes and large black zippered bags around the boat.

A girl with long, frizzy brown hair and puffy eyes glanced away when I came up. I could tell she'd been crying. A short stub of a kid with blond hair and blue eyes picked at a scab on his knee.

Delphine, sitting cross-legged next to Micah, whispered something to him and they both glanced over at me, laughing, as if sharing an amazing secret. It seemed like they had known each other for much longer than today.

I walked over to them and sat down with a sigh.

"Care to fill me in?" I asked.

"Speak of the devil, it's Reed . . . Reed Mackenzie, right?" Micah asked, looking at me with a smirk. I didn't say anything. "Delphine just told me your dad is Tim Mackenzie."

Wow, that didn't take long, I thought, feeling annoyed.

"Well, is it true?" he asked.

I glanced around to see if anyone else was listening in, but it appeared no one else was paying attention to us.

"Yeah, I recognized your dad right when he walked up," Delphine chimed in. "Even with those horrible sunglasses and that God-awful baseball cap."

I couldn't help but laugh, which instantly gave me away. They *were* terrible—I'd been saying that for years.

"Was that supposed to be a disguise or is he just that much of an asshole in real life?" she asked.

I was so used to people worshipping the ground my dad walked on that Delphine taking him down a notch caught me by surprise.

"He's *that* bad. The whole culture guru thing is a sham," I joked, and Delphine giggled while Micah shook his head in disbelief. To me, this was partially true. My dad's public persona and how he was at home felt like two different people entirely. "He gets all of his amazing ideas from me, actually," I said sarcastically. Of course this was a lie, but it made Delphine grin. Her smile was wide and addictive—a smirk that started in her eyes and continued down to her lips.

"Shit, get out of here," Micah said. "Your dad is the man and you know it." He then laughed heartily and I joined in. Right away, I could tell he was one of those people that was impossible not to like.

"Okay, dude. Whatever you say," I responded,

shrugging him off. I was relieved that there were at least a couple of cool kids in the program.

Just then, a loud horn pierced our conversation and I jumped, making Delphine snicker.

We turned to face Titus, who was holding a megaphone to his lips and looking down at us from a platform above the deck. The two crew members flanked him—their thick necks and crossed muscled arms bulging out of their matching red polo shirts.

"Time to get moving. Everyone excited?" Titus boomed through the megaphone, which seemed unnecessary for a group our size.

"Oh yeah! Let's do this!" I yelled out, and managed to get a small laugh from the group—even the crying girl.

I wondered where we were headed and what we would do when we got there. The Ship Out brochure hinted about working on the boat itself and volunteering in exotic locales around the world, but didn't go into specifics, which seemed strange.

Everything was glossed over and put into new age, therapy bullshit bullet points. I wondered if my parents knew more—the vagueness of the info packet made me uneasy now that I was here, staring out at the endless expanse of sea.

"Actually, I have a question," I called to Titus. Everyone turned to look at me.

"Reed?"

"So, where are we going, anyway? Do we have an itinerary?"

These seemed like perfectly legitimate questions to me, so I was surprised when the crew members behind Titus laughed, shooting each other looks, like I told a joke in which they already knew the punch line.

"Of course we have an itinerary," Titus said.

I stared at him, waiting. He stood there silent, grinning down at us.

Finally, I asked, "Well, are you going to share that with us?"

"No," he shook his head. "I'm afraid not."

"Why not?" I demanded.

Titus sighed, and then smiled again, even wider and more forcefully this time.

"Dr. Wingett's Ship Out philosophy is based on the principle that when one surrenders wholly to the process of this journey—without knowledge of what is next or where we're heading—a primal discomfort grows that will force each and every one of you to turn inward and build reserves of strength and maturity that never existed previously," Titus spoke slowly, looking around at each of us, letting those words sink in fully.

He continued, "Because really, that's what life is about. You think you have your shit together and WHAM! You get hit with something you never, ever expected or planned for." We all sat silently, like no one knew what to say. Finally, Titus spoke again.

"Isn't that right, Reed?" he asked, speaking into the megaphone, staring down at me and not looking away. I wondered if he was referencing what happened to my brother.

It was in the news—of course he knew about it, I realized. He probably studied files crammed with all the ugly details about my life and my issues, paperwork my mom likely filled out when applying to the program.

I met his gaze, unwilling to give him the satisfaction of acknowledging I understood what he was implying.

"Asshole," I heard Micah utter under his breath, and Titus either pretended not to hear, or didn't care. He continued speaking.

"Weak, undisciplined people fold when faced with adversity or when things don't go as they had hoped. They turn to drugs or crime or allow depression to overtake them."

He made a point of taking time to look each of us in the eye while he was talking.

"This journey is all about the unexpected. And we'll demand you rise to the challenges you face. If you do so, I promise you'll shake off those demons that are holding each of you back."

As Titus talked, the two guys behind him frowned with tight-lipped scowls.

"Okay, okay . . . enough," I said. "We get it. It's really hot. Can we get this whole thing over with already?"

The blond kid with the scab glanced over at me with wide eyes, and cracked a very small smile.

Three months sounded like forever—I was going to miss out on so many parties that my friends had been talking about all year. And I was already hot and uncomfortable and I felt the familiar tug of craving a beer or a swig of vodka pulling at my brain. How could I last three months without having a drink? That felt impossible.

"Sure, Reed. If you're *so* eager to leave your old life behind, I agree, let's go," Titus said, looking at me with a frown. He and the crew stepped down and began untying the thick yellow ropes connecting the boat to the dock.

"What a jerk," Delphine said to me as she squeezed a glob of sunscreen into her hand and rubbed it in sloppy streaks over her face. White lines painted across her nose and forehead.

I laughed. "You got a little something extra there," I said, pointing to her nose.

"Well, then, why don't you help me with it?" she demanded playfully and I felt myself blush. I reached out and smudged the stripes with my fingers until they were gone.

"Aw, Reed, thanks," she said, looking at me with a smirk.

"That's what friends are for, right?"

"Get a room," Micah piped in, and Delphine laughed, shoving him away.

As we started to pull away from the dock, I tried to look calm, but the idea of being out in the middle of the ocean on a boat with no way to communicate home felt creepy. I'd had a tablet and a wristlet since elementary school and was used to being able to reach anyone I wanted—at any time—through a few verbal cues or a press of a button. Being out at sea, without any devices, sounded both scary and lonely, but I didn't want to let on that I was nervous.

Just minutes later, the marina was far in the distance and there were no other boats in sight. We bobbed lightly up and down over calm waters. A few seagulls flew overhead and cawed at us and then eventually, even they scooped away out of sight.

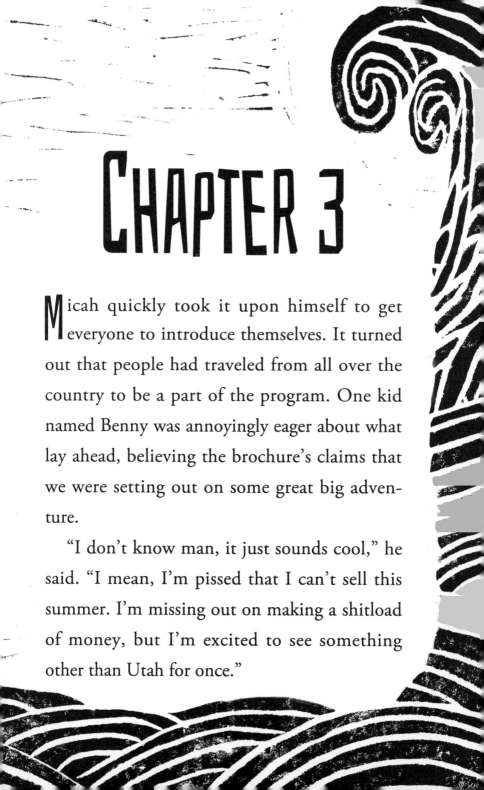

CHAPTER 3

Micah quickly took it upon himself to get everyone to introduce themselves. It turned out that people had traveled from all over the country to be a part of the program. One kid named Benny was annoyingly eager about what lay ahead, believing the brochure's claims that we were setting out on some great big adventure.

"I don't know man, it just sounds cool," he said. "I mean, I'm pissed that I can't sell this summer. I'm missing out on making a shitload of money, but I'm excited to see something other than Utah for once."

"Drugs?" Trevor asked, perking up, and Benny nodded.

"Yeah, me too . . . " Trevor said and they slapped hands together. Trevor continued, "But do you know where the money's really at?"

Benny shook his head.

"No idea. What's that?"

"Identities. Stealing them in batches of thousands, hundreds of thousands—and selling them online to the highest bidder."

"Really, man?"

"Yeah, that's where it's at. You just need to be careful. My dad figured out what I was doing and look where I am now. I got sloppy," Trevor said, shrugging. "But I can tell you how to do it, if you want. We have the time," he said, and Benny eagerly agreed.

We then learned that Rose was caught with a trunk full of uppers in her bedroom, and that Carl's sister was a bitch because she ratted him out, but he wouldn't say what about exactly.

"What about you, Delphine?" I asked. "Why are you here?"

"Cuz I tried to kill myself," she said and gestured with her hands like she was hanging from a noose.

"Oh Jesus, I'm sorry!" I said, feeling weird and sheepish about talking about something so personal.

"Geez, Reed—aren't you gullible?" Delphine snorted, and burst into a fit of laughter. "Don't believe everything a girl like me tells you," she joked and everyone giggled along with her. I wondered what that meant, but before I could press, Delphine turned her attention to Micah.

"It's a really boring story, compared to all you nut jobs. It's not even worth talking about," he said, refusing to say more even when I prodded. He smiled and turned to me. "You're up."

"Hi guys, I guess Titus already introduced me, but my name is Reed."

"He's Tim Mackenzie's son, like *the* Tim

35

Mackenzie," Micah blurted out and I glared at him. I really didn't want everyone to treat me differently, but that seemed inevitable now. "Isn't that awesome?" he said, smiling at me with a goofy grin.

I saw the other kids sit up almost at once, staring at me with a sudden curiosity, and a few chimed in with "ooh" and "really?"

I nodded, feeling my face flush red. Micah slapped me on the back good-naturedly, like he was making sure there were no hard feelings.

He came across like a natural leader. I wondered why he was on the program—he seemed to have it all from where I was standing. But, maybe, because of who my dad was, people thought the same about me too.

As we sailed further and further out to sea, we joked around with each other and told stories about our lives back home while Titus and the crew members tended to the ship.

There were two girls in the group, Rose and Delphine. Each was attractive enough, but Delphine was definitely the one that caught my eye. She was an equal-opportunity flirt, and she flitted about the group, smiling and laughing every time someone made a joke like it was the most hilarious thing she'd heard in her life. Her infectious laughter rose up over the sound of the waves and I couldn't help but notice the other guys in the group noticing her. Immediately I sensed she was different from the girls I knew back home—and I was eager to get to know her better. Maybe this boat wouldn't be so bad after all, being stuck in such tight quarters with her.

As she stepped back in my direction and latched arms with me, I was excited to talk to her again. But just then, Titus and the crew members came over and stood before us.

"Gather around," Titus ordered and we all

reluctantly ended conversations and moved from our spots spread across the deck to a tighter circle around him. I hung back, still feeling the sting from our earlier interaction.

"This is True," he pointed to the tall, muscular guy on his right, who hovered at least a foot over even Micah. True nodded and frowned at us. He wore mirrored aviator glasses and it felt like he was watching me, even though his eyes were obstructed.

"And that's Sully," Titus gestured at the short one on his left, who was shifting his weight from his left foot to his right, like he had to take a shit or something.

"The three of us are your captains, your counselors, your teachers, and your judges for the next three months," he spoke slowly and deliberately, punctuating each word as he scanned the group. "You do what we say, when we say it, and I promise this will be a much more pleasant experience for you."

He talked with a friendly tone and that large smile—a tall row of white teeth and a fixed stare—but it was obvious to me his words were meant as a threat.

"Believe it or not, I was in your shoes once. With no direction and getting into trouble all the time. I stole credit cards. I used drugs. I dealt drugs. I didn't care for anyone else but myself," he said, his mean eyes boring into us.

Here we go, I thought, biting my tongue to keep me from telling him I'd heard this speech many times before. These therapy pep talks always had the opposite of the desired effect on me. Back home, I'd leave a therapist's office and immediately find a new and inventive way to get into trouble.

"I know what it's like to not have a higher purpose, to be a ship with no rudder or sail—unable to progress or pivot. It is a terrible affliction," Titus continued, his expression turning sad. True and Sully nodded.

"You have a golden opportunity with the Ship Out program to turn everything around before it's too late. Before you're in jail or worse," he said. I wondered what was worse than jail. Being stuck on a small boat for three months with these new age blowhards as our overlords sounded close to me.

Titus continued, "Tomorrow, you'll receive your job assignments on the ship, but today, we get to know each other a bit and break bread. First, let's go down to the living quarters," he ordered, turning on his heel to head down a steep staircase that was directly behind him, leading into the belly of the ship.

Everyone moved slowly, our bodies not acclimated to the rocking of the boat. Delphine shot out her arms to catch her balance and others followed suit. We looked like drunks. I wasn't particularly eager to comply with Titus's commands, so with my duffle in hand, I stopped to turn and stare out at the water, an infinite blue sheet rolling slowly toward the late afternoon sun.

"Let's go," a voice yelled from behind me, and I felt a hand nudge me hard on the shoulder. I swung around to find True glaring at me. "Believe it or not, the world doesn't revolve around Reed Mackenzie," he said. I looked at him and he puffed up his chest and stepped into me.

I hadn't done anything to challenge the Ship Out crew except ask where we were going. I sighed. "So this is how it's gonna be?"

"You don't know the half of it," True snapped, and a large wave suddenly heaved under the boat, tipping it to the right quickly, and knocking me off my balance and onto my knees. True remained upright as if standing on dry land, and he laughed. "Let's go, pretty boy," he said, grabbing my forearm and pulling me up.

"Back off, I'm moving."

I tried to recover like it was no big deal, but after my tumble, I felt like an idiot. I sensed True's eyes on my back as we stepped into the steep, narrow staircase that led to the boat's living quarters.

The staircase opened up into a cramped room with shiny, wood-paneled walls and cushioned benches that lined the perimeter. The area was small with low ceilings, and the group was squished together tightly. The air was a heavy mix of sweat, saltwater, and cologne, and I gagged a tiny bit, wanting to run back upstairs to take a gulp of fresh air.

The hacker kid with the shaggy hair, Trevor, was greenish all over, and I could tell just by looking at him that he was going to throw up any minute. He curled up on a corner bench and I thought he might start crying.

I decided to stay as far away from him as possible.

The rolling motion of the waves combined with the incessant rocking of the boat did take some getting used to, and I felt on the brink of puking myself.

I gripped the bottom stair's railing and collapsed into the one remaining open bench, right next to where Titus was standing. He smiled, completely unfazed by the motion of the boat, or the smell, or by how many of us were squeezed into such a small, hot space.

It was dark, except for the sunlight that streamed through the small portholes along the walls, and I glanced over at Delphine, whose red hair glowed like a halo from the sole beam of sun that shone on her back.

"This is the common area, with the galley over there," Titus said, pointing to his left at the kitchen. "Behind me, that's the hallway to the crew rooms. If we even sniff any one of you anywhere near that hallway or our quarters, you will be in a world of trouble and won't see daylight for days, I promise you that," he said and turned his head to look down at me.

"And over there are your living quarters," he shifted to face a very cramped hallway that led to a handful of narrow doors, painted shades of the rainbow.

He rattled off names and pointed to different doors, and the group dispersed as everyone headed to their rooms to drop off their stuff.

"And last but not least, the real trouble makers, Reed, Micah, and Carl, you'll be in room number three," he pointed to a door at the end of the hall that was painted a bright, happy purple. It was jarring against the dark wood paneling and fluorescent lighting of the hallway.

I felt relieved that I was rooming with Micah, but didn't know much about Carl yet except that he hated his sister. Other than that conversation, he'd spent the entire afternoon picking at that massive scab on his knee, not talking to anyone.

"Okay, drop off your stuff, get cleaned up, and meet us back upstairs in five," Titus ordered before he departed up the stairs.

Micah, Carl, and I squeezed through our door and I checked out what would be our room for the next three months. It was a glorified closet with a few beds and a bathroom.

"Yikes, tight quarters, huh?" Micah said, dropping his bag on the narrow single bed on the left side of the room. "Dibs."

"Soooo . . . Tim Mackenzie's kid. Wow," Carl said, shaking his head in disbelief, staring at me with his mouth open.

"Yep, it's true," I said, trying not to roll my eyes as I looked over at Micah, who was smiling widely.

"That is so cool. He's one of my idols . . . seriously!" Carl said and I stared dumbly at him, not knowing what to say. Oh great, a fan boy. I hated these conversations.

"Well, what's he like, like, at home?" Carl asked, unable to hide his excitement.

"He's a real dream, considering I'm here and obviously an upstanding young citizen," I joked.

"Yeah, right?" Micah said, and we laughed together.

"You got a point . . . " Carl responded, looking a little disappointed. Blood slowly oozed out of the gash in his knee, but he didn't seem to notice. I sat down on the lower bunk.

"But seriously, what's he like?" Carl asked again. The kid had no shame.

My dad was the founder of Yu-Du, an internet search engine he built in his parents' basement many years before I was born that became *the* site people used to find anything about everything.

Although he wasn't immersed in the day-to-day business any longer, he'd become something of a cult hero to geeks, shut-ins, and business leaders around the world. He'd spent my whole life traveling around the world delivering inspiring talks to large, rapt crowds about everything from the future of technology to entrepreneurship to meditation. I'd joke with my friends that people would probably pay thousands of dollars to listen to my dad talk about mice shit—and that he'd do it, if the price was right.

Being at home and seeing him every day in his holey sweatpants, eating cereal, and spilling dribbles of milk on his tablet, it was easy to forget he was famous. And whenever he talked to me, he imparted 'wise' thoughts through generic sound bites as if I were an adoring fan, instead of trying to really get to know me, his teenage son.

When I wouldn't volunteer any more information about my dad, Carl moved on with a shrug. "I'm short. I'll take the top bunk," he chimed in and threw his bag with one arm over my head and onto the upper mattress.

A few minutes later, in the hallway, we met up with everyone else.

"Let's get upstairs, guys. It's been longer than five minutes," Rose said nervously.

"Chill out," Micah joked. "What are they going to do—throw us overboard?"

Everyone laughed.

I noticed Trevor hanging back, head down. I let the others shuffle back and put my arm around him. "Aside from the sensation that I might barf at any moment, this doesn't seem so bad, right?" I asked. He looked up. His face had lost all color and he was trembling.

"Too late for me," he croaked, wiping at his mouth with a sour look.

"Yeah, gross dude," the jacked Asian kid named Benny called back. "He threw up all over our bathroom. It reeks."

"You okay, man?" Micah asked, helping me prop him up as we got to the top of the stairs.

Sully and True were waiting for us.

"Titus said five minutes," True said, looking down at his watch. "That was ten. So, that's fifty push-ups for each of you . . . ten for each minute you were late," he ordered, and we all groaned. It seemed hardly possible to do even a single push-up with the boat tilting so sharply to the right and left.

"I can't do push-ups," Rose, the puffy-eyed girl cried. "I've never done one in my life."

"Time to learn. Get down NOW!" True yelled at her. I could tell he meant business and so I decided to get them over with rather than complain and draw more attention to myself. As I got down on all fours, I nearly toppled over as the boat lurched into a wave trough. A blast of sea soaked us.

"True?" Trevor asked, hesitating. He was clinging to the staircase railing for dear life. "I'm really sick . . . I literally just threw up downstairs. I can hardly walk."

"And?" Titus interjected, looking at Trevor, confused. He wasn't amused. "That's not going to stop you from joining in. Get down," he said, pushing down on Trevor's shoulders. Trevor crumbled to the deck on his knees, weakly moving up and down and straining to lift his body weight off the wet, wooden deck.

On all fours, I struggled to complete the fifty

as the ocean rocked the boat. I glanced over at Micah, who was casually pumping out push-ups like it was no big deal.

Later that night, after we all dried off, we were assigned shifts in the galley to help make a dinner of canned meatballs, spaghetti, and stale garlic bread.

We brought the food up to the deck and sat cross-legged to eat off plastic plates. The waves had calmed and the moon cast a glow over the boat, its giant sails gleaming in the light. I couldn't fully relax as I felt the gaze of True, Sully, and Titus on us as we ate. They sat just feet away in metal folding chairs—listening in as we talked about our lives at home—and occasionally whispered things to each other.

Delphine was very quiet next to me and I noticed her pasta went untouched. I remembered that in the galley earlier, she told me she was a vegetarian, so I snuck extra slices of garlic bread onto her plate. She smiled at me and I felt a rush of momentary happiness.

After dinner, I was exhausted. I wanted nothing more than to crawl into bed, but Titus made us mop the deck and scrub dishes first. Whenever I got close to Rose—who was trying to look busy blotting at a spot on the ground that I wasn't certain actually existed—I heard her sniffling.

As I stood nearby, Delphine came up and leaned down to Rose.

"Psst . . . don't let them hear you cry," she said, and quickly handed Rose a piece of toilet paper.

Rose glanced up and grabbed it, wiping at her nostrils and looking grateful for the gesture. Before she had a chance to say thank you, Delphine moved away, shuffling with her mop to the other side of the boat.

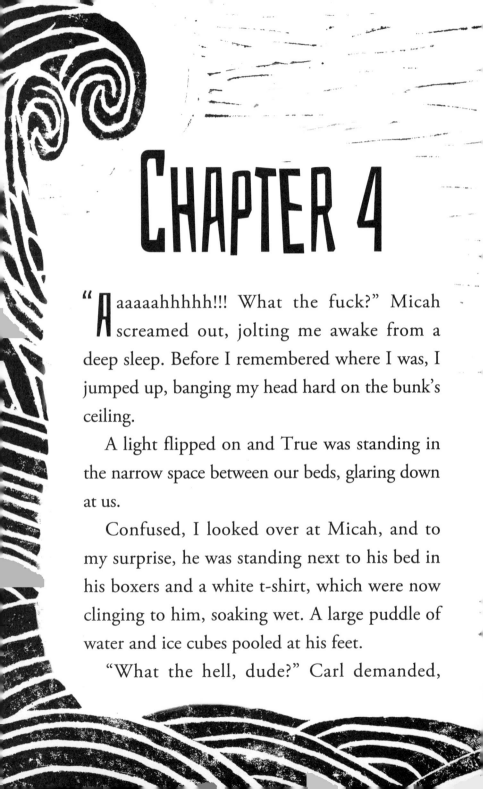

CHAPTER 4

"Aaaaahhhhh!!! What the fuck?" Micah screamed out, jolting me awake from a deep sleep. Before I remembered where I was, I jumped up, banging my head hard on the bunk's ceiling.

A light flipped on and True was standing in the narrow space between our beds, glaring down at us.

Confused, I looked over at Micah, and to my surprise, he was standing next to his bed in his boxers and a white t-shirt, which were now clinging to him, soaking wet. A large puddle of water and ice cubes pooled at his feet.

"What the hell, dude?" Carl demanded,

swiftly hopping down from his bunk, pushing around me and getting in True's face. He was a lot shorter than any of us, but was built like a bulldog, stocky and strong.

"You have something you want to say to me?" True asked. "Go for it and let's see what happens," he said.

Carl's face was turning a shade of bright red and I noticed his misshapen ears for the first time as they flushed purple. A fellow wrestler, I realized. He stood still for a moment, contemplating his next move, and Micah suddenly spoke up.

"Chill out, Carl. It's not worth it," Micah said as he took off his wet t-shirt and waved Carl back from True.

"You're right." Carl mumbled, backing down, and sitting next to me at the edge of my mattress.

"So, do you have something you want to say to me or not?" True pressed, taunting him.

"No," Carl said, glaring at True.

"No . . . what?"

"No. True?" Carl guessed.

"No *sir*. I'm actually surprised that a guy who viciously attacked his own sister isn't crazy enough to push back," True spat out with a disgusted look on his face.

Carl stared at him with huge eyes, surprised, and then glanced over at both Micah and me.

"What? It wasn't like that. I didn't attack her," he cried out, standing up again.

True moved forward and got in Carl's face. "I know *all* about you, Carl. I know all about each of you," he said, looking dismissively at me, and then at Micah. Carl became quiet and appeared shaken up.

"Now get upstairs," True ordered.

"Dude, calm down," Micah said angrily. "That wasn't necessary. What is this about?"

"You're right. It's not necessary." True said, his bug eyes bulging under the bright white light that swung overhead. "But, you'll soon find that our behavior modification methods are very effective."

Micah backed down ever so slightly.

"Now, go up and get to work," he ordered, prodding at Micah as we moved toward the door. I heard muffled yells in the hallway.

The three of us shuffled down the hallway, running into Delphine and Rose. Delphine was also soaked, her pink tank top clinging to her skin. She looked at me, and I thought I could make out fear in her eyes for the first time.

"What's going on?" she whispered to me as we started up the staircase.

"No idea," I said, shrugging. At that moment, I was suddenly reminded of Titus's words about throwing the unexpected our way. It was night one and we were already getting roughed up. This is going to suck, I thought, trying to brace myself for whatever test they were about to put us through.

When we stepped out onto the deck, we came upon Trevor, Benny, and Marcus, who were kneeling just a few feet away, the moonlight illuminating their faces. I could tell Trevor had been crying.

"Get down," Titus barked, and True pushed me hard with both hands, knocking me to my knees on the deck. Micah got down on his own, but Carl stood firm, refusing to move.

True tried to shove Carl down, but Carl swung his body out of the way, causing True to trip forward before he recovered and charged at Carl.

"No!" Carl yelled. And as if something snapped inside him, he lunged forward, pushing at True with both hands, who stumbled backwards and fell hard onto his butt.

I heard Delphine laugh out and I glanced over, shaking my head at her to stop.

Titus suddenly stepped forward in between Carl and True. Before I could process what was happening, Titus lifted a metal rod in his hand, flipped a switch with his thumb, and swiftly pressed the instrument against Carl's back. To my surprise, a bright electric blue bolt zapped out of the device, causing Carl's whole body to shake and collapse instantaneously. The weapon made a loud hissing sound, like a bug being caught in a lamp, and Carl screamed out in pain.

Rose cried out "Oh my God," and everyone else gasped, but no one got up to challenge Titus further.

Sully stood back with his mouth open.

"What the . . . ?" Carl gasped, glancing up at Titus with shock, and scrambled to stand back up, when Titus swung out his arm again swiftly, zapping Carl once again, but for longer this time. Carl yelped in agony and I couldn't take it.

Before I could second guess myself, I jumped up and grabbed at the instrument in Titus's hands. His mouth was open wide with surprise, and he swung the metal rod at me. I caught it before he could turn it back on and wrestled it from his grip. Without giving it another thought, I took the device, which was hot to the touch, and flung it as far as I could into the ocean. The dark metal flew through the moonlight before it landed with a loud plop in the water.

I knew immediately I'd made a dumb decision. Titus stomped over to a metal chest under a bench, pulled something out of it, and turned back, charging in my direction. Before I could determine where to run on a sailboat with no hiding places, I felt a jolt of electricity shoot through my body. As I collapsed, I looked up to see Titus angrily holding another metal instrument against my chest. It felt like a fire was careening through every corner of my body and I screamed out, the pain far worse than anything I'd ever experienced.

Sully stepped forward, alarmed.

"What are you doing, Titus?"

As Titus turned to look at him, I saw hatred and anger overtaking his face. Sully stepped back, like he second-guessed questioning his leader.

Crumpled on the ground, I couldn't move and stared out at everyone who was kneeling around the deck. Each person was very still, afraid to budge even an inch. I saw Carl on the ground past Delphine—he was curled in a fetal position and not moving, either.

Titus put the rod back in the metal chest, and turned to address the group, his face glowing a pale blue under the moonlight.

"This is what happens when you don't follow the protocol of the Ship Out program," he said, putting the tip of his boot's heel on my chest, which vibrated in pain.

"Unfortunately, this was an example of Reed throwing good money after bad, you get me?" I could see Titus's smile gleaming.

Everyone was silent. "You see, Carl was the one who fucked up, right? But Reed thought he'd be the hero," he said as he sneered down at me, pressing the weight of his boot into my sternum. "And hero is a job he's not well suited for, actually."

He kind of laughed to himself and True joined in. Sully frowned but didn't interject.

"I've got news for you. There are no heroes on this boat. You are all mine for the next three months. You understand? You do what we say when we say it, and we won't have another night like tonight, okay?" Titus said, scanning the group for agreement. "And if you do what we say when we say it—you get better. It's that simple. You go back home and live as future-functioning members of society, okay? So get your shit together and follow our commands. You understand?"

Everyone nodded, although I could see a mixture of fear and anger in the faces among the group.

"We don't care if you've never worked a day in your life. You got me?" Titus was looking directly at me. He took his weight off of my chest and reached out a hand to lift me up.

"Yes, sir." I said. I felt too weak to stand, but didn't want to give him the satisfaction of collapsing again.

I thought back to the images of the smiling kids

in the Ship Out brochure, waving at the camera from the bow.

I couldn't help but wonder if this abusive treatment was actually part of Dr. Wingett's protocol—the real reason why parents had to sign non-disclosure agreements and why there was no communication back home once the boat left shore. Hey, if a kid came back in better shape than when they departed, then was a little tough love so bad?

But I knew if my parents had any idea what was actually happening, they'd be appalled and my dad would sue the shit out of Dr. Wingett and everyone else involved with Ship Out. He'd put the program in the ground.

I felt a tiny bit of satisfaction knowing what a colossal mistake my parents made sending me away. I couldn't wait to get home to say "I told you so."

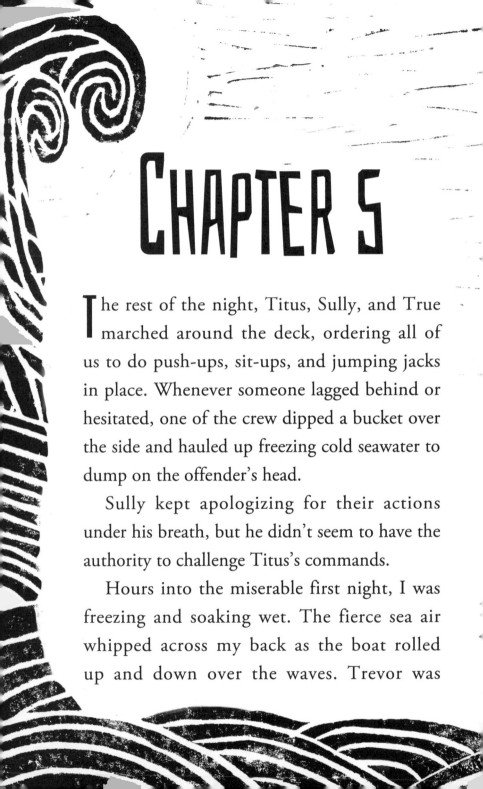

CHAPTER 5

The rest of the night, Titus, Sully, and True marched around the deck, ordering all of us to do push-ups, sit-ups, and jumping jacks in place. Whenever someone lagged behind or hesitated, one of the crew dipped a bucket over the side and hauled up freezing cold seawater to dump on the offender's head.

Sully kept apologizing for their actions under his breath, but he didn't seem to have the authority to challenge Titus's commands.

Hours into the miserable first night, I was freezing and soaking wet. The fierce sea air whipped across my back as the boat rolled up and down over the waves. Trevor was positioned next to me, and he threw up repeatedly. Each time it happened, True tossed a fresh bucket of water over Trevor's head, sending the vomit to the edges of the deck, where it would eventually wash over the sides.

I wasn't sure how long we'd been there, but I gathered it had been three or four hours before the sun began to peek up over the horizon.

"Okay, I think that's enough. I'm bored," Titus finally yawned into the megaphone. "Time to get up and get to work! Go down and put on some new clothes."

I felt weak on my feet and wanted nothing more than to crawl downstairs, take a hot shower, and collapse in bed.

"Now you know what Ship Out is really about," Titus said as we trudged toward the staircase. He had a coffee mug in his hand, which he sipped loudly before smacking his lips. I glanced around at my shipmates; everyone was soaking and visibly shaken up.

"That is one sick fuck," Micah whispered to me as we squeezed down the stairs, and I couldn't help but laugh just a little bit.

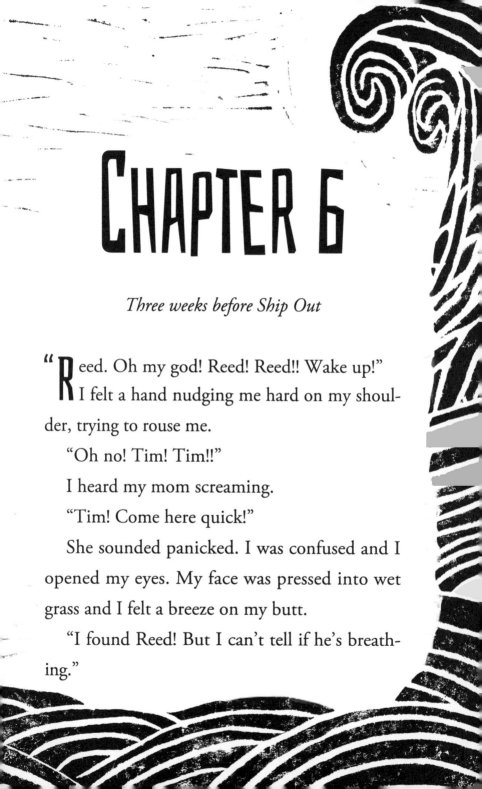

Chapter 6

Three weeks before Ship Out

"Reed. Oh my god! Reed! Reed!! Wake up!"
I felt a hand nudging me hard on my shoulder, trying to rouse me.

"Oh no! Tim! Tim!!"

I heard my mom screaming.

"Tim! Come here quick!"

She sounded panicked. I was confused and I opened my eyes. My face was pressed into wet grass and I felt a breeze on my butt.

"I found Reed! But I can't tell if he's breathing."

Her voice was far away and I didn't understand what was happening.

Where was I? I attempted to lift my head, which throbbed under its own weight, and I groaned loudly, letting it flop down again.

I was in my backyard. I could see the sliding glass door through the blades of grass, but I couldn't figure out why I was there. Something moist trickled into my ear, causing noises to seem very distant and everything to echo.

"Oh . . . thank God. Tim!" She screamed again and I heard a door opening in the distance.

"What is going on?"

My dad's yell ricocheted around the inside of my head, his voice suddenly very close. I felt a hand on my back and my dad's head was next to mine. He looked at me closely.

"Ugh . . . " I protested, swinging my arm out, trying to push him away. I wanted to go back to sleep.

"He's bleeding." My dad called back toward

my mom. "Reed—get up right now!" He pulled me upright, and I looked around. The ground felt sloped beneath my feet—I was definitely still drunk.

"Oh my God," my mom cried out when she saw my face. "I'm calling 911," she said as she started to head back into the house.

"You are doing no such thing!" My dad screamed at her. "Do you know what a mess that would create? Don't you remember? Just what we need—"

He yanked me under my armpits to keep me from falling down.

"Let's bring him into the house. He's okay. Right, Reed?"

"I'm okay," I grunted in agreement, although my eyes were nearly glued shut and it felt like my head and body had gotten hit repeatedly with a bag of rocks.

My mom came over and helped my dad by grabbing me on the other side to lift me up as we all hobbled inside. She ran to grab towels from the closet and threw them down on the couch.

I collapsed onto the cushions and groaned loudly. I looked down and realized that I was completely naked. My dad, as if he was reading my mind, threw a towel over the top of me. In the moment, it seemed like the kindest thing he'd ever done.

"Do you know where you are?" he demanded.

"Yes, we're at home," I mumbled, looking at him through slits.

"How many fingers am I holding up?"

He thrust his hand in front of my face and held out four fingers.

"Two?"

I couldn't help myself.

Through my swollen eyes, I saw my mom's face. It was filled with terror.

"Hahaha . . . just kidding you guys . . . it's four."

I was trying to make a joke, but my dad was furious.

"This isn't funny, Reed. What happened last night?" he asked.

The honest truth was that I had no idea. I knew we started the night at Anthony's house and broke into his parents' liquor cabinet. We poured vodka and gin into red plastic cups, and then replaced the contents of the empty bottles with water.

I then remembered leaving to go to a party at a senior's house, and making out with a small blond girl outside.

The last thing I recalled clearly was walking down the street with her.

But how did I get back here?

And why was I bleeding?

I didn't know the answers to any of these questions.

My mom came over with a wet rag and started wiping at my face, which made me moan in pain. Even though I still felt alcohol coursing through my body, the rag against my skin was excruciating.

My mind raced as quickly as it could to come up

with a reasonable excuse for what happened, but I was sluggish.

"I was at Anthony's last night—we watched a few movies—and then I walked home—and then I wanted to look at the stars—so I fell asleep out there—" I offered, but realized that didn't explain the bleeding. Crap.

"You're lying to us, Reed," my dad said. "Again. I can't say I'm surprised anymore."

"It's the truth," I murmured, closing my eyes and resting my head against the couch cushion.

"Okay, then how do you explain this," he said as he stuck his hands under each of my armpits and hoisted me up. The towel fell away and I felt embarrassed that I was standing before them naked. He dragged me down the hallway and we walked into the bathroom together.

When he turned on the light, I looked up at the mirror.

"Oh shit," I said, when I saw my reflection. My whole face was different shades of purple and red, and my eyes were nearly swollen shut. I had a long cut along my right eyebrow, another gash over my nose, and a huge, bloody scrape on my cheek.

I was nearly unrecognizable, and because I still felt drunk, somehow this was funny to me and I couldn't help but laugh out loud.

"I'm going to ask you just one more time, Reed. How did this happen?"

He sounded more furious than concerned.

The honest answer was that I had no idea. I must've blacked out, which was becoming a common occurrence. It was obvious someone beat the shit out of me, but I had no recollection of fighting anyone.

"Hey . . . if I look like this, I wonder what the other guy looks like?" I joked, and my dad stormed away, leaving me to slouch down to the bathroom floor and curl up in a ball. I grabbed at a towel hanging from the rack, and covered myself with it like a blanket. This was a fine enough place to go back to sleep.

As I started to pass out, I heard my dad say to my mom, "I think it's time I talk to Jorge about that program."

I faded away to the sound of my mom quietly cursing me as she hunched over my body, wiping at my face.

Chapter 7

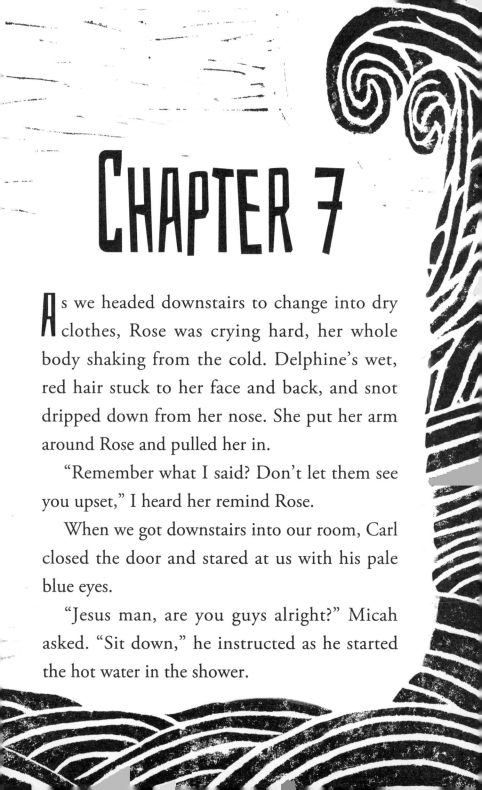

As we headed downstairs to change into dry clothes, Rose was crying hard, her whole body shaking from the cold. Delphine's wet, red hair stuck to her face and back, and snot dripped down from her nose. She put her arm around Rose and pulled her in.

"Remember what I said? Don't let them see you upset," I heard her remind Rose.

When we got downstairs into our room, Carl closed the door and stared at us with his pale blue eyes.

"Jesus man, are you guys alright?" Micah asked. "Sit down," he instructed as he started the hot water in the shower.

"Yeah, I'm okay. I can't wait to get back at those fuckers, though. Just you guys wait. They'll wish they'd messed with someone else," Carl muttered, his face pinched in anger.

"Just don't do anything stupid," I warned. After seeing a glimpse of what Titus was willing to do to us, I didn't think it was smart to provoke him further.

"What the hell was that about, anyway?" I wondered aloud.

"That, my friends, is what it's like to be scared straight," Micah said as he got into the shower.

A minute later, he hopped out and came into the room to finish getting dressed. "My guess is that they're going to do whatever they can to break us so that when these three months are up, we'll be begging to return home. And then, when we get back, we'll promise our parents we'll never, ever fuck up again."

He spoke with nonchalance, like he'd been through this exact situation before.

"Yeah, kind of like those forest programs where they drop kids off in the middle of the woods," I said, thinking back to Jeremy from my school.

"Exactly. I did one of those two years ago and look where it got me," he said, shrugging at his surroundings.

"But we can't let them break us. This isn't right. What Titus did up there has gotta be illegal, right?" Carl asked, his face flushed with anger.

Micah shrugged. "Well, not much we can do about that at the moment."

He continued, "But do you know what will really drive Titus crazy?"

"What?" Carl asked.

"Not giving them the satisfaction of reacting at all," Micah said. I was surprised by how casual he was about the whole thing.

Micah kept talking, "I just don't let people get a rise out of me. Parents, my girlfriend, teachers, whoever—it makes them nuts that I just don't care. It's almost like a game to me. I've found the less I react, the easier it is to get my way."

"Yeah, you're right," Carl said. I nodded too but I felt uneasy.

After we all got changed, we stepped into the hallway and Sully was waiting for us.

He glanced up at the stairwell. "Listen, last night got out of hand," he spoke quietly. "I'm not sure why Titus did that. This is my first time sailing with him or True or Ship Out, actually, and Titus is a bit more . . . intense than me. But, he's my boss, so you know, I do what he says," he said, sounding nervous.

Sully hesitated and turned to make sure no one else was coming. "Ultimately, I believe in what the program is trying to accomplish, and Dr. Wingett's philosophy and practices. And, I was told Titus is one of the best Ship Out practitioners around, so you know . . . "

I couldn't help but roll my eyes.

"So when I tell you to do something, just do it.

I don't want to have to punish you even more," he said, looking at Carl, who averted his gaze.

"Now let's go up and have some breakfast." He motioned for us to follow him, then knocked on the others' doors. Everyone piled out of the rooms and we stood in a cramped huddle together, no one eager to go back upstairs. Standing in the back, I saw Sully put his arm around Delphine to comfort her. She cringed, pulling herself away forcefully.

"Is that part of my therapy?" she asked, narrowing her eyes.

Sully frowned. "Geez. I was just trying to be friendly."

Weeks of the same routines and torture passed with no new updates on where we were heading. Because he liked to harass me most of all, I was assigned to cleaning bathrooms every day.

"Here you go," Titus said to me with that irritating smile and handed me the red toothbrush. It wasn't the one to clean my teeth, but rather, to scrub the boat's four toilets. It was a dirty and disgusting job on a ship with questionable plumbing, and since we'd been on the boat, Titus made me polish the toilets every single day. After I was done, he'd closely examine my work and if a bowl wasn't clean enough to lick (his words), he'd punish me with push-ups, wall sits, and other grueling physical tasks. Bruises lined up and down my forearms and calves from hitting the deck countless times.

Everyone took turns doing other tasks—cleaning and maintaining the boat's deck equipment, ropes, galley, and rooms—but the toilets were all mine, despite my protests. Today, I felt annoyed about the situation and just wanted off the boat and back onto land. I was sunburned, hungry, continuously exhausted, and off-kilter, and I wasn't learning anything here except how to try to evade Titus, True, and Sully's attention.

"Feeling crappy, Reed?" Delphine stood next to me as I was about to head downstairs with the toothbrush. She had a smirk on her face. I didn't respond as I knew where the conversation was headed and I tried not to crack a smile.

"It's a shitty job, I know," she continued, and Micah, who was standing nearby, piped in.

"Yeah, Reed's in the dumps these days," he said, causing Delphine to giggle.

"He always looks pooped."

This was their thing, coming up with really bad puns about my job cleaning the toilets. They liked teasing me as much as they liked making each other laugh. I tried not to join in, but often laughed with them as our situation *was* ridiculous. I never in a million years thought I'd end up on a sailboat, on my knees, scrubbing shit stains off toilets and trying not to gag.

Delphine teased me like I was her brother, and even though she was cute, given the circumstances, our relationship felt like a friendship and nothing more.

As each day passed, Carl, Micah, and I became closer, and spent the evenings after lights out discussing in detail our favorite movies and music—rehashing memorable scenes and lyrics, talking about girls, and plotting unrealistic ways to escape the boat or exact revenge on Titus and his crew.

Carl's fuse was very short, and he often lashed out within the confines of our room about how we were being treated. One day, he punched a dent into the thin wall next to our bed, which we covered up with pillows whenever we left the room. Titus hadn't used the metal instrument that shocked me since our first night, but we didn't want to tempt him.

A few times after I'd fallen asleep, I'd awaken to hear Micah get up and leave our room for a while. Carl never seemed to notice—he slept deeply, snoring loudly each night.

When I'd ask Micah about his middle-of-the-night departures the next day, he'd fess up that he liked going up to the top deck to get fresh air. We were forbidden from leaving our room after bedtime.

"Don't tell anyone," he'd say and I'd agree, not wanting to get him into trouble.

"Of course not, man."

"It's what keeps me sane."

And when he said that, and smiled at me like we were sharing a secret, I got it.

After four weeks on the boat, everyone was growing impatient—weren't we supposed to be stopping in remote locales to volunteer? We all wanted off the boat badly, but when we asked about our progress and when we'd be on land again, Titus would always say, "Soon enough, soon enough . . . " and nothing more.

This morning felt different from the get-go. Titus seemed in an especially good mood when we came upstairs, greeting us with a loud hello. After a sad breakfast of sticky, flavorless oatmeal, he came over to the group to make an announcement. He leaned both arms on the table and looked down at us with that huge grin. "Today is a big day in the Ship Out program," he said, and True nodded, while Sully appeared surprised.

"It's Ocean Day, which means each of you are going to take turns jumping in."

He gestured over to the water and looked back at us.

"You mean . . . in the ocean?" Benny asked. He seemed a little dumb every time he opened his mouth. Titus nodded.

"Of course, where else?" he asked.

"You have to be joking," I said, as I couldn't help but chime in, hoping this was just one of Titus's lame attempts to scare us.

"Oh, I do? Do you consider me to be a joker?"

he asked, looking at me with that irritating smile. I shook my head. I hadn't swam since my brother's accident and I felt my whole body tighten up in fear.

"Now Reed, since you're challenging me, I think you're on deck to show 'em how it's done. Get to the edge," he said, nudging me toward the side of the boat.

"It'll just be a quick dip. We'll throw out the life ring for you, don't you worry," Titus offered. True moved to stand on the bench next to the ship's edge, holding the ring in his hand, ready.

Micah looked at me and shook his head back and forth. I couldn't tell if he was trying to tell me not to resist or that this was just a scare tactic, and that I should act cool and indifferent.

"Now, get up there," Titus ordered, pushing me up toward the boat's slippery ledge, metal instrument in hand at the ready. I feared both the pain that that device could inflict and the water that was zipping by below.

I stood up carefully on the railing and my legs shook.

"Please don't make me do this," I said quietly, turning back to look at Titus, who was smiling at me.

"Oh, I'm afraid you don't have a choice," he said, holding up the rod like he was about to strike me. I glanced down, considering my options. Both filled me with terror.

"And, I tell you, you gotta face your fear of the water at some point, right?" The words stung and I swung around to confront him.

"What does that mean?" I demanded.

"I think you know what I mean," he said, and I felt my face turn bright red. I wanted to jump on top of Titus and strangle him.

But, before I could help it, tears welled up in my eyes. His words were a slap that brought memories of James's accident rushing back in an instant. I hadn't cried in front of anyone since his service. I quickly wiped away at my eyes but I knew everyone saw. As I glanced over, I caught a glimpse of Delphine's lips pinched in a frown.

"Okay, Titus, enough is enough," an angry voice snapped behind me. I spun around, surprised to see it was Sully speaking up, moving toward Titus. "This surely isn't part of the program!"

Titus turned and stepped toward Sully with the metal instrument raised. Sully flinched but stood his ground to challenge Titus. Instead of getting angry, Titus took a deep breath and stared coolly at Sully for a long moment before speaking.

"I'm getting tired of you questioning my authority. You better think twice before talking to me like that again, understood?"

Sully nodded, but I could tell he was angry. Titus continued, "But you're right, Sully. I just wanted to test Reed, per the program's philosophies," he said, shrugging before he turned back toward me. "I wasn't going to *actually* make you jump in the water . . . obviously. That's incredibly dangerous. You think I'd want to kill you?" he asked, laughing at the suggestion. True snickered but Sully was quiet.

"Now, get down and join the others," Titus ordered, pointing to where everyone else was gathered, staring at me. Titus shook his head like he was surprised he had gotten that reaction out of me.

CHAPTER 8

Two nights later, Titus surprised us once again with news about the next leg of our journey. "One more sleep and we'll be at our first destination. We'll be re-stocking the boat's supplies and volunteering as well. That's when you'll see just how lucky you have it," he said, looking over and making eye contact with True.

After our confrontation a few days prior, I knew in my gut they were toying with us. But everyone else was so excited about the prospect of leaving the boat and getting on land again, I kept my reservations to myself.

That night, Micah and Carl tried to guess

where we were heading, while I lay in bed thinking about home and my friends.

"What's up man, why so quiet?" Micah asked as he prepared for bed.

"Just a little homesick, I think," I said.

"Well, not too much longer and we're free. And, it looks like we'll have a change of scenery soon enough," he said as he lay down in bed.

"Yeah, we'll see," I replied and closed my eyes, not wanting to talk about where we might be going the next day. I didn't have a good feeling about it.

That night, the sound of the waves crashing against the hull mingled with my roommates snores and I couldn't sleep.

I wondered if my parents knew where we were, or where we were heading. I was hurt that my mom agreed to send me away, and couldn't believe that they'd put me on a boat, of all things. That led to thoughts about James, and I pushed at those memories, making them disappear to the furthest corners of my mind.

Next, I pictured Delphine and recounted our funny conversations, like I often did late at night when I was trying to fall asleep. I had a feeling that Micah liked her, but he would never admit it when I asked.

CHAPTER 9

It was very late when I finally dozed off to sleep, the rocking of the boat working its inevitable way with me.

Soon after drifting off, a loud BANG BANG BANG woke me up. I sat up quickly and looked around.

"What is that?" Micah asked, but I couldn't see him in the darkness.

Many times since our journey began, the crew suddenly woke us up in middle of the night to subject us to various physical tasks, but this sound was different.

"What's going on?"

Loud foot stomps echoed above us. I then

heard the footsteps coming down the stairs at a furious pace. Someone was running down.

Our door swung open and I could barely make out the silhouette of a person wearing a black mask. The hall light was off, which was odd. The man was carrying what appeared to be a gun in his hand, but I couldn't tell for sure.

"Ha, ha. Very funny, guys," Micah joked. "What sort of drill is this now?"

"Get up to the deck . . . immediately!" The voice barked at us and it didn't sound like Titus, True, or Sully to me.

I heard muffled screams and stomping above us. I knew better than to resist or move slowly at this point, so I got up and felt Micah and Carl pushing behind me, rushing to get out the door.

"This is a bit much, isn't it?" Micah asked the guy, who was at Carl's back.

"Move!" the man ordered again, and I strained in the dark cabin to see what was going on. There were more bodies in front of me in the living

room area as everyone strained to get up the stairs quickly. I heard Marcus and Benny yelling protests, but I could barely make out their silhouettes.

When we got to the deck, the lights there were also off, and the man with the gun shoved us over to the side where a group was huddled in the darkness. I heard a few more men yelling, and I tried to re-focus my eyes to see who it was and where we were being pushed.

Soon, I made out the shapes of Rose and Delphine coming up the staircase. "We're moving, we're moving. Chill out."

It was Delphine, and she sounded more annoyed than scared. The man at their backs grunted something that I didn't understand.

He pushed the girls in our direction and Delphine fell into me. I caught her small body in my arms and she laughed nervously. "Thanks. What the hell's going on?"

"Just another scared-straight tactic," Micah said under his breath, and sighed loudly, annoyed.

"And I thought I'd seen it all. I'm absolutely exhausted. Can we go back to sleep and do this in the morning?" he asked.

In the darkness, I barely made out someone standing before us and that he was wearing a ski mask, but I couldn't see clearly who it was. The man spoke up.

"Time to get moving. You're all de-boarding this ship now," he ordered. He definitely didn't sound like any of the crew members.

"Why? Where are we going?" I heard Trevor's voice, but I couldn't see him.

The men pointed flashlights to the side of the boat and I saw something was attached to the railing that hadn't been there before.

One of the men pushed us forward, the beam of the flashlight swinging back and forth, barely illuminating our path. The group took steps forward slowly, tripping over each other and whispering about where we could be heading.

I strained to listen to the men, who were speaking in urgent tones.

"Dude, this is ridiculous. Titus is really taking things too far now," Micah said. We were all sick of being woken up in the middle of the night.

"So, I guess we're heading to our first volunteer location?" Benny chimed in, from behind me. No, that didn't seem right.

At the edge of the boat, everyone's bodies pressed around me.

"Now you . . . climb down, now!" one of the men barked at the first person in line, who I could tell was Trevor by the dim outline of his shaggy hair. The man pointed the flashlight downward at a rope ladder that was hanging over the boat's edge. I spotted more flashlight beams crisscrossing the night sky, their origin a large motorboat below. I heard a loud boat engine revving and the smell of gasoline filled the air.

Rose was next. "But I'm scared of heights," she whined, her voice trembling.

"Move now or we'll toss you over ourselves," the man ordered.

"Okay," Rose said, then whimpered loudly with each step she took downward.

Next was Benny, then Micah, then Marcus. I could barely hear them as they each boarded the boat below, the motor sounds drowning out their voices.

When it was my turn, I had a sick feeling in my stomach. I still couldn't clearly see the face of each man in the darkness, but something didn't feel right. None of these men sounded like our crew, and the guns were extreme, even for Titus.

I felt the cold metal tip of a gun pressing against the small of my back and I looked down at the ladder.

I contemplated protesting, but couldn't think of a possible resolution that ended well for me.

I climbed down the rope rungs, which wobbled and swayed with each step. Finally, I got to the boat, and one of the masked men grabbed my hand and yanked me down to a metal seat.

In the darkness, I couldn't see anyone, except when the flashlights' beams crossed near our faces.

As we sat there, the boat bobbing underneath us, I heard the muffled voices of men talking over our heads, on the sailboat. The people were speaking angrily to each other.

I thought I heard Sully, but I wasn't sure. The motor was so loud.

"I'm . . . not . . . going . . . with . . . you!"

I swear that's what the person said, but I couldn't be certain.

All of a sudden, there was a splash directly behind us, and I felt icy water hit me in the face. It seemed like something large and heavy had been tossed in the ocean.

Micah laughed. "This is rich."

"What's going on?" I asked.

"Another messed-up way to get us to shit our pants and do whatever they say," Micah said. "I can't wait to get home to rat out this asshole," he grumbled.

"Yeah," Marcus agreed. "I just want to go back to sleep."

To make myself feel better, I tried to believe that Micah was probably right, given what we'd been subjected to already. Titus seemed to relish finding new ways to torture us.

Several people climbed down the ladder and jumped into the motorboat in rapid succession, causing it to rock violently back and forth.

"Time to get going," a man said loudly with an Australian accent. He definitely wasn't any of the Ship Out crew.

We suddenly felt untethered from the sailboat, and soon we were speeding across the water, the boat slapping up and down over the waves. Each time we crossed one, a large splash came over the bow, hitting me in the face like a slap. Before long, I was soaking wet and freezing.

All I could hear was the loud hum of the boat's

engine, the waves crashing around us, and each person periodically screaming out as a cold wall of sea spray washed over the boat. For just a moment, I thought I heard Titus talking, but couldn't tell for sure.

It felt like we'd been on the boat for hours. My butt and back were sore from the hard seat and being jostled roughly so many times.

I tried to convince myself that where we were headed had to be better than this. How could it be any worse?

Chapter 10

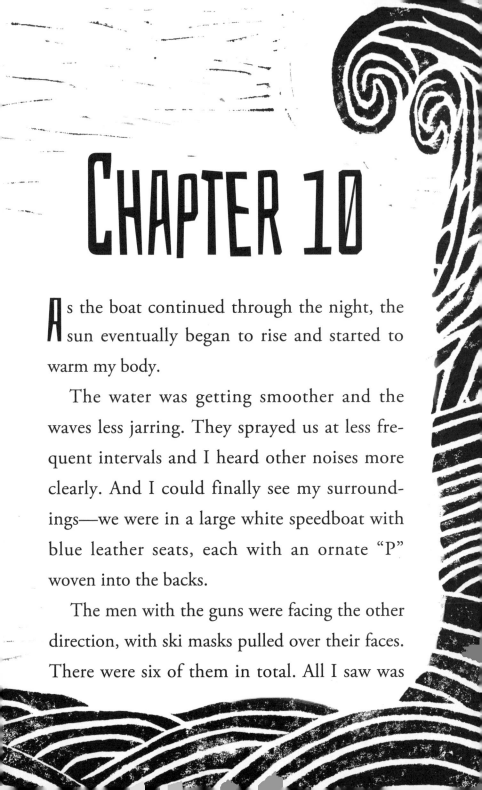

As the boat continued through the night, the sun eventually began to rise and started to warm my body.

The water was getting smoother and the waves less jarring. They sprayed us at less frequent intervals and I heard other noises more clearly. And I could finally see my surroundings—we were in a large white speedboat with blue leather seats, each with an ornate "P" woven into the backs.

The men with the guns were facing the other direction, with ski masks pulled over their faces. There were six of them in total. All I saw was their backs, and from this angle, I had no way of knowing who each of them were.

"We'll be there soon. Send a message to Gareth we'll be arriving by seven," the man with the thick accent said to the taller man on his left. "Make sure the preparations are ready."

"Yes, of course. Right away," the man responded. I thought this person might be Titus and I craned to hear him speak more, but he was now silent.

Delphine leaned against me. "What do you think is going on?" she asked.

"Maybe the next stage of the program?" I offered, but truthfully, I had no idea. I was totally confused, but that was a normal occurrence on the Ship Out program—constant disorientation at the hands of the crew.

Soon, seagulls cawed and the water became very calm compared to the hours before.

The chill of the water was still in my bones, even though the sun was out.

"Okay. Okay. Who's ready for breakfast? You have a big day ahead of you, so it's time to eat," the man with the Australian accent said as he moved away from the wheel, handing it off to the tall man. His eyes were dark in the ski mask, and I couldn't make out who it was.

He got up and pulled a large paper bag and a thermos out of a plastic case that had been strapped to a ledge along the inside of the boat.

He turned to the front row, where Benny and Marcus were sitting, and pulled a bagel and a doughnut out of the box.

"Choose one . . . or both," he said, nudging the food at Benny, who eagerly took one of each. "And a cup of coffee, of course," he offered.

I could've cried tears of joy. A doughnut sounded like the most perfect food ever created and he couldn't get to me fast enough.

When he approached Delphine, next to me, she said to the man, "No coffee please. I hate the stuff."

"Well, then . . . may I offer orange juice?" he asked kindly and she nodded. He grabbed a small plastic carafe from his case and poured her a large glass.

When he stood before me, I eagerly took a glazed doughnut, a bagel and a cup of coffee and gulped it down, even though it was too hot. It was the most spectacular taste and I couldn't help but say "aaaahhhh" as it went down smoothly.

Micah laughed at me as he took a sip out of his cup.

As I finished mine, I was tempted to ask for another when I saw a large expanse of land come over the horizon. At that distance, it was nothing more than a green and mountainous mass and our boat was heading straight toward it.

We all became excited, yelling and pointing at the island. "What is that place? Where are we?" Rose cried out, and suddenly, her words began to slur. "I feel weird . . ."

I also felt strange, like being on a bad trip, and when I stood up, my legs buckled under me.

I saw Delphine collapse in a heap on the boat floor and then Carl, and then Marcus.

I looked up at the man with the accent and he stared down at me through the eyeholes in the mask.

"It's working," he said, glancing over his shoulder at the tall man whose back was to me during the boat ride. As the world got fuzzy, the man turned his head and I thought I saw Titus's blue eyes gazing at me.

The last thing I remember was Micah lunging at the man, and soon, everything faded to black.

CHAPTER 11

I woke up to the sound of Micah screaming. "Let us out of here right now!"

I opened my eyes and found myself laying on a mattress covered with clean white sheets. I turned my head, taking everything in. I was in a small room with stone floors and metal bars on three sides. The front faced a large circular area, and there were other "rooms," or cells, lining the edge of the circle.

I heard moaning behind me and I swung around to see Marcus laying on the other bed. He was passed out but starting to stir.

"Micah?" I yelled, not seeing him immediately.

"Over here!" I heard him yell and looked around to locate him. He was leaning against the metal bars of the cell across from mine, sticking his arms out to try to reach the door's latch unsuccessfully.

"What's going on?" I yelled out to him, and then looked around at the other cells. In some of them I spotted bodies strewn across mattresses, while others seemed empty. I heard snoring and labored breathing coming from the different enclosures. My head throbbed painfully and my body felt wobbly on its feet.

"They drugged everyone," he said. "It must've been in our drinks," he guessed as he looked around to see if anyone was coming. "I only had a few sips, so I've been awake for a while."

"Where are we?" I asked. The last thing I remembered before passing out was spotting a large, green island as we approached it, and Micah jumping toward the man on the boat.

"I don't know. I haven't seen anyone else. I

think there are two of us per cell. I'm with Benny. He's snoring like crazy right now," he said.

"Is this part of the program?" I wondered aloud.

"Probably. It has to be, right? Maybe they're trying to recreate what it's like to be in prison?" Micah said.

"Oh yeah, remember how Titus said we'd all end up in jail?"

I recalled Titus's warning and wondered if he was testing us again.

"He'll probably come out and start yelling at us at any moment, boot camp style," Micah said.

"Yeah . . . my head fucking hurts . . . ouch . . . " I replied as I sat back down on the mattress. Just then, Marcus opened his eyes, looked at me, and then sat up quickly.

"What's happening?" he demanded. He got up and clumsily lunged in my direction. "Where are we?"

"I don't know, man! Sit down before you fall

over," I said, guiding him to the bed. He collapsed on it again.

We sat there quietly for a few minutes, with the silence interrupted periodically by Micah yelling at the top of his lungs, trying to get someone to come into the room.

"Hello?"

"Titus! Sully! True! Come out!" He screamed out. "Come out!"

As we waited for them to arrive, everyone in their cells began to stir, groaning in pain, and calling out for Micah, whose yelling was waking each person up, one by one.

Micah reassured everybody as they moved toward the front of their cells. I couldn't tell if he actually believed that we were okay or if he was just doing his best to fulfill his role as our de facto leader.

"What's going on?" Delphine asked.

She was two cells away. She leaned her head against the bars and turned to make eye contact with me. She was biting her lip and I could see she was trembling. I smiled hoping to comfort her, but I'm sure she could read the fear in my own face.

Just then, the metal door leading into the main circular area swung open and a tall, thin man with bleached-blond hair and wearing an all white suit strode in, and stood in the center of the room.

"Hello everyone. Good morning!" He talked in a chipper tone, like the circumstances we found ourselves in were totally normal.

"Where are we?" I asked, my head still throbbing. "Where's Titus? Did you drug us?"

He looked at me amused. "Wow! So many questions! I love your curiosity!" he said as he walked around, tapping his left hand on the bars of each cell as he passed.

"Yeah, sorry about that. You guys must all feel terrible right now, huh?" He asked, looking genuinely concerned.

"Why were we drugged?" I asked and he turned to look at me.

"Well, it's our protocol whenever new visitors come here, we must ensure that the island's distinguishing characteristics are protected. In these circumstances, that really seems unnecessary, but the rules are the rules," he sighed, shrugging to himself.

"And where's Titus?" I demanded. I was suspicious that he wasn't here with us. "And who were those men on the boat?"

"Oh don't you worry about Titus. I'm your new guide," he said. He paced back and forth. Rose shrunk back as he passed her cell.

"I don't actually use this," he said, sensing her fear, as he waved a club in his right hand back and forth. "It's just for show, really."

"My job here is to take care of you. To make you comfortable. To ensure you eat heartily and sleep well. Think of me like a counselor," he said.

"So, who are you?" Micah asked, and the man turned to him.

"Oh, that's right. Forgive me," he pushed his

wireless glasses up his nose. "I'm Darby. Pleasure to make your acquaintance."

Everyone stood and stared at him, waiting for him to continue.

"Well, first order of business, we eat. And this is very important. You'll need to build your strength in the coming weeks. Bring it in, White Suits," he spoke into a wristlet-like device and just moments later the metal door swung open and several more men walked in, each carrying a tray of food.

They were all wearing identical white outfits— pressed white slacks, a neat white polo shirt with a form-fitting white blazer on top. And, each wore a small white cap pulled low, nearly obstructing their eyes.

One by one, each man went to a cell door, punched in a code, and entered an enclosure. When a man came to our cell, he dropped off the tray, not making eye contact, then promptly left again, locking the door behind him.

I could smell the food from where I sat and my

hunger roared back all at once. It was a savory, meaty scent and I walked over and removed the metal cover from the tray. A golden roasted chicken, mashed potatoes, French bread, butter, and a side of chocolate cake were arranged across the plates. I suddenly felt a lot better, and starving.

Remembering what happened with the coffee, I hesitated, even though I wanted to rip the chicken apart right away.

"How do we know you didn't lace this again?" Micah asked, his eyebrows raised.

"Well, that's not in my best interest now," Darby explained, and walked over to enter Micah's cell. "Like I said before, I'm here to take care of you and make sure you get the training and sustenance you need to succeed."

He was standing before Micah, his warm disposition a welcome change from how we'd been treated the last couple of weeks by Titus and his crew. Despite myself, I couldn't help but believe him.

"Would it make you more comfortable if I took a bite of each of your food items, and a sip of your drink?" he asked, looking at Micah for a reaction.

"Yes," Micah said, and Darby reached down, picked up the fork and knife and proceeded to have a large bite of the chicken, then the potatoes, then the bread and butter and last, the cake. He then took a huge gulp straight from the water pitcher on Micah and Benny's tray.

"Amazing! Our chefs are among the best in the world. You won't be disappointed. Now eat up," Darby said, handing the fork to Micah. "You have a big day ahead of you."

Now that the drugs had worn off, my headache was replaced by irrepressible hunger and I imagined everybody else felt the same. Everyone began to rise from their mattresses and moved over to the tables in their cells.

The food was so delicious I couldn't help but moan when I took the first bite. The chicken's crispy skin concealed a moist, juicy breast and

I consumed my portion in less than a minute. Everyone else commented on how amazing the food was, and Darby went from cell to cell, peeking in.

When he got to us, he smiled and said, "Oh, so glad you all enjoyed. There's more meals like that in your future. I promise you won't be disappointed."

I stared up at him. "So, where is Titus again? And what about True and Sully?"

"It's time to move on from them—from the boat—onto the next stage of your journey. Now's when the real challenges and opportunities for growth begin," Darby explained, and his answer made me feel uneasy rather than better.

"So is this the volunteer portion of the program?" Marcus asked, looking suspicious.

"Sure, you can call it that, as long as we use a loose definition of the word 'volunteer,'" Darby said, smiling at us.

Seeing the confused look on my face, he then

said, "You'll figure it all out soon enough, my friend."

"Now, time to get into your training attire," Darby ordered, as he exited our cell, shutting the door behind him. He spoke loudly, addressing the group as a whole. "There's an outfit for each of you in your dressers. Get ready now and we'll take you to your next location." He walked over to the girls' cell and pulled down a thick curtain so they could get dressed privately.

I went to a small metal dresser that was bolted to the floor and pulled out the outfits for Marcus and me. All I found was a small pair of white shorts for each of us.

"This is it?" I asked incredulously.

"Yes, sir. I know it's not much, but it does the trick," Darby said.

Marcus and I got dressed and stood there awkwardly, waiting.

"Now, let's get moving." Darby went over and removed the curtain blocking the girls' cell and then unlocked each cell door. Delphine and Rose were standing there, now wearing nothing more than white sports bras and shorts. Suddenly embarrassed, I looked away, not wanting Delphine to catch me looking at her.

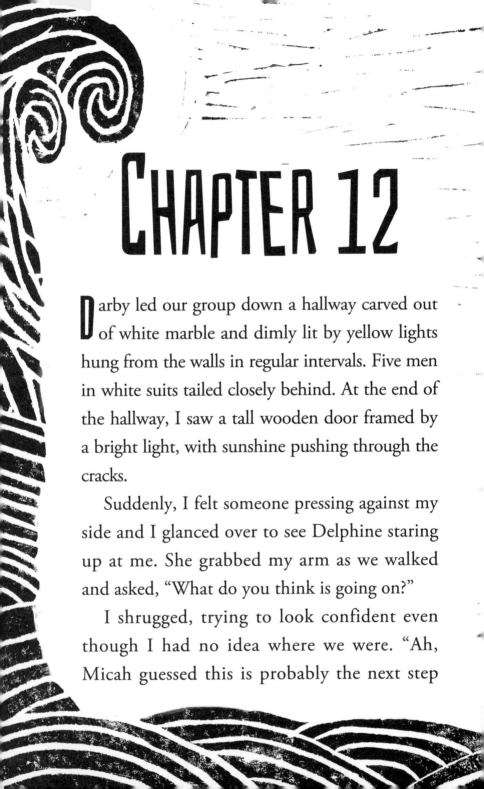

CHAPTER 12

Darby led our group down a hallway carved out of white marble and dimly lit by yellow lights hung from the walls in regular intervals. Five men in white suits tailed closely behind. At the end of the hallway, I saw a tall wooden door framed by a bright light, with sunshine pushing through the cracks.

Suddenly, I felt someone pressing against my side and I glanced over to see Delphine staring up at me. She grabbed my arm as we walked and asked, "What do you think is going on?"

I shrugged, trying to look confident even though I had no idea where we were. "Ah, Micah guessed this is probably the next step in our program. That makes sense, right?" I said, but the words didn't sound true coming out of my mouth. She looked at me with her eyebrows raised.

Darby swung open the door and I was suddenly blinded by the sunlight. He stepped outside and beckoned us with a long, slender hand to follow. "Well, come on everyone, don't be shy," he said.

Micah stepped out first and then the group pushed though, with Delphine and me walking out side-by-side. As my eyes adjusted, I looked around, trying to get a bearing on our surroundings.

We were in a large courtyard, flanked on the sides by tall marble columns and stone walls. There were large windows cut into the stone high up on the walls, for what I couldn't figure out. The ground underfoot was a mix of chewed-up grass and dirt, and on the far side of the courtyard there were several oversized chairs lined up, each covered with velvety purple cushions. No one was

sitting in them at the moment, but they seemed regal, and I wondered who they were for.

Darby stood about ten yards from our group as we huddled closely together. I felt exposed standing shirtless there. I looked up at the windows. Suddenly I realized what I was seeing—someone was watching us. A chill ran down my spine. Who was watching us? And why?

Darby addressed us, "Now the real work is to commence, my friends. Strong Men, please come out." He called toward another door carved into the wall to the left of us. Immediately, it swung open and two men walked out, each lean and muscular. They were wearing white tank tops and white shorts, and their skin gleamed under the sun.

"Friends, these are the Strong Men, Ames and Max," Darby smiled at the guys that stood beside him, their arms folded across their chests.

"They're here to get you ready for the challenges you'll face soon enough," he explained and

I glanced over at the other kids, the confusion on each person's face clear.

"They're going to make you work very hard, but those who work the hardest will be best prepared for what's next," Darby said, looking at the group. "That's all I'm allowed to say at this point, but please trust me when I implore you to take this all very seriously," he said, before pursing his thin lips.

"I must go now, but I'll be back at the end of the day to take you back to your quarters," Darby continued, and before we had a chance to ask any questions, he promptly turned and disappeared through the door we'd all come through, with the five nameless White Suits, as he'd dubbed them, following close behind.

"Hello recruits!" the shorter, tanner Strong Man spoke up with an Australian accent, and I immediately recognized his voice from the speedboat.

"M'name is Ames, and that's Max." Max nodded at us politely, but didn't say a word.

"Before we begin, I want to tell you something important. We cannot hurt you—in fact, our whole job is to make you stronger, faster, and smarter—but if you disobey us or don't follow orders, you go in the Hold with no guaranteed release—solitary confinement, you understand?" Ames said, and we all nodded.

"I gather you were treated pretty badly on that boat, weren't you?"

I had to say something that was bugging me.

"You're the guy who drugged us, aren't you?" I asked. I was sure it was him. He didn't respond to the question and kept on talking.

"Things are different on my watch, trust me. I'm going to make you work hard, but I won't physically demean you, okay? Now let's get going with something easy—why don't you drop and give me fifty push-ups? I want to observe each of your conditioning," he said.

"What's this about?" Micah asked, but Ames just shook his head and didn't say anything. He pointed at the ground.

A few people grumbled complaints, but we each got down to the grass and did our best to get through the push-ups quickly. We'd been conditioned to understand resisting would be punished immediately.

Ames turned to Max. "Not bad. Especially that one and that one and that one." I couldn't see who he was pointing at as I pushed through the exercise. "That one over there—yikes, there's a lot of work to do there. No upper body strength at all," he said. As I finished, I looked up to see Max taking notes on a tablet he was holding.

"Okay, now time to test that agility," Ames explained, and went to a metal closet at the side of the courtyard and retrieved jump ropes for each of us. "Let me see what you can do. Whoever successfully jumps the longest without a break can be done with training before everyone else today," he said.

After years of conditioning as a competitive wrestler, I had jump roped thousands of times and was confident in my abilities. We all started skipping the rope and some of my fellow 'recruits' failed quickly, their feet getting tripped up in the cord within a minute. I continued, confidently jumping and doing double unders to show everyone I meant business. I looked over to see Carl also hopping up and down effortlessly, along with Rose, to my surprise, making it seem easy.

"Woah . . . Rose . . . who knew?" I yelled over as I continued to jump, starting to feel a bit winded.

She looked over at me and laughed. "Was a national double-dutch champ for four years," she said, talking easily like it was no big deal, not out of breath in the least. For some reason, this made me laugh and I got tangled in my rope. Everyone exclaimed "ooooh," and I caught Marcus smirking at me.

Carl, since he was also a wrestler, appeared comfortable for a few more minutes, but then succumbed to exhaustion, throwing down his rope angrily before collapsing on the ground to catch his breath.

Rose was the victor. Her face was flushed red and she grinned, the happiest I'd ever seen her.

For several hours, we were put through several other physical tests gauging speed, stamina, strength, and in some cases, determination. Ames and Max watched over us—not barking orders, but making it clear that the activities weren't optional. Max continued to take notes on the tablet throughout—furiously tapping away as he observed us. He and Ames whispered periodically, and nodded to each other when someone excelled at a given task.

It was exhausting—but it was also surprisingly kind of fun—especially compared to the torturous conditions of the sailboat. Throughout the training we joked with each other, playfully teased when someone faltered, or congratulated when someone's physical abilities surprised the group— as was the case with Rose and the jump rope.

Ames and Max encouraged the camaraderie that we displayed, and occasionally joined in as well, making jokes and helping everyone feel at ease, despite the mysterious circumstances of this training.

Although each person had their own strengths, it was clear who the athletes among us were. Carl was small but fierce and excelled at nearly each test set forth. Micah was a beast—his tall, lean body was all muscle and confidence, and he strode through each test easily, hardly becoming winded when the rest of us collapsed on the grass gasping for air. I also had my strengths, but got tired quickly, and realized partying non-stop the last two years had taken its toll on my body.

At one point, we were challenged to toss a

heavy rock as far as we could. Right when I was about to throw it, Delphine yelled out, "Just imagine that's Titus's head!"

Everyone laughed, including Ames and Max. I smiled over at her, lifted the rock, and launched it forward with all of my might. Everybody cried out as it landed with a heavy thud past where even Ames and Max were standing. Delphine yelled "Show off," and I looked over at her to smile. She was cute, standing there in her sports bra, her hair tied in a loose braid resting on her shoulder.

As the sun began to set, Darby came through the door and looked at us. "Well, it appears like it's been a successful day," he said. Ames and Max nodded.

"This is a good group. They show a lot of promise," Ames said. "We've sent the notes to you and Gareth, but I think everyone will be pleased," he explained to Darby, who smiled widely.

"Wonderful news. Well, everyone, I imagine you're famished. Who wants pizza?" Darby asked.

We all cheered, and headed back as a group to the cell area, where White Suits brought us steaming hot pies with oozing cheese.

At the end of the night, Darby shut off the lights and we all yelled out in the dark to each other, telling jokes and guessing what we'd be doing the next day.

That night, I dreamt of my brother. I saw him in the water, flailing, and reached out my arm. He grabbed onto it and no matter how hard I pulled, I couldn't lift him out. The water splashed around him for what felt like hours, time dragging out so each second was multiplied by ten. Even though I was dreaming, I told myself to wake up. I gasped out loud and bolted upright in the bed, my whole body shaking.

I looked around and it was very dark—I could scarcely make out Marcus in his bed, but I heard his heavy breathing, along with the snores and sighs of everyone else sleeping around me.

There was just a sliver of moonlight coming

through the windows high up on the room's tall walls.

I looked over and thought I spotted a woman's silhouette standing outside the cells. It was like a shadow.

"Hey! Who's that?" The person moved quickly and opened the door leading to the hallway, slipping out and shutting the door behind her before I could say anything more.

"Dude . . . who are you talking to?" Marcus asked from his bed, awakened.

"I have no idea," I said and then lay back down, feeling uneasy as I tried to fall back to sleep.

CHAPTER 13

I ran out into the early morning sun, completing the wind sprints Ames made us do every day after breakfast. We'd been on the island for two weeks and I was starting to get my wrestling lungs back. Running felt good, and each day's sprints and long jogs around the training floor cleared my mind.

Every day, I thought less about alcohol, drugs, and the parties I was missing back home, and I started to feel healthy and focused. I didn't understand the circumstances of the training, but the outcome seemed like it was doing what Ship Out promised—rehabbing my head and body after two years of constant abuse.

We were put through grueling physical tests for hours, led by Ames and Max, who treated us firmly, but with kindness. Even though they wouldn't say what we were training for, to my own surprise, I worked hard to impress them, to have them tell me "Good job," or to catch Ames saying something nice about me, and Max writing it down in his tablet.

Ames seemed to focus on me more than the others. When I'd wrestle against Carl, or practice fencing maneuvers against Benny, Ames would come over and share detailed pointers, but barely give them advice. During water breaks, he took me aside for pep talks.

"He likes you—like, really likes you," Delphine joked, and I shrugged. Maybe he did? Truthfully, I was flattered by Ames's attention as it felt like he saw something special in me. He reminded me of my favorite wrestling coach growing up.

During these first weeks on the island, the only outdoor time we got was in the courtyard and we didn't ever volunteer helping poor kids, as the Ship Out brochure promised. We all agreed that whatever was happening wasn't what we expected from the program, but we weren't being tortured of verbally abused, so it didn't seem so bad, compared to the alternative.

One day, as we were starting the morning's training, I saw out of the corner of my eye someone slip through the door and go sit on one of the velvet purple chairs that were positioned just off the training floor.

I hadn't seen visitors since I'd noticed the shadows watching us on that first day. Who could that be?

I looked over and spotted the most beautiful girl I'd ever seen. She perched on the chair's edge, wearing a loose, white blouse, and her skin was tanned, like she had just returned from a tropical vacation. A cascade of dark hair fell around her shoulders and she tossed it nonchalantly the moment I glanced her way. She smiled, and I looked away, embarrassed. Ames and Max nodded her direction, also smiling.

"Hello there," she said to them.

"Welcome, Chelsea. Glad you could join us," Ames said in return. She sat back in the chair, making herself comfortable, and pulled out a magenta fan and started to sway it in front of her face.

Who was she, and where did she come from? I saw the other guys in the group staring slack-jawed at her. I think it was safe to guess she was the most gorgeous woman any of us had ever seen in real life, and it was obvious we were all distracted by her presence. I caught Delphine's eye for a moment and she quickly glanced away, looking annoyed.

As Chelsea watched us, Ames and Max told us it was time to start incorporating grappling into our workouts. Grappling? Like what I used to do in wrestling practice? This should be easy for me, I thought, feeling confident.

"Reed and Marcus, you'd be a good match-up, why don't you go first," Ames directed, and I stepped out to the center of the courtyard, where Marcus also joined me.

I looked at him and smirked. "You up for this, man?"

I snuck a glance in Chelsea's direction. She clapped in approval.

"Yeah, why wouldn't I be up for it?" Marcus responded defensively. He didn't like me, but I couldn't pinpoint why. We circled around each other, bent over, arms at the ready. Marcus grinned at me, but his eyes were cold.

Ames stood just a few feet away, and I heard Benny and Trevor calling out, cheering us on. "Let's go, guys. One of you make a move," Trevor yelled.

I circled slowly around Marcus again, and when I saw his eyes dart toward Chelsea, I ran forward and lunged at his legs, picking him up and throwing him down to the ground onto his back. I quickly collapsed my body on top of his and put all of my weight on his shoulders to pin him down. He struggled to squirm out from under me, but I was too strong.

As I was doing it, I realized that I stayed on top of him a few moments too long, and that I had pinned him *too* easily. I was trying to impress Chelsea, and everyone else.

I felt arms pull me off of Marcus, and push me away. "Great job, Reed," Ames said, and then reached out a hand to Marcus to lift him up. Marcus got up, his face beet-red, and he wouldn't look at me.

"I just got lucky," I offered, trying to smooth over the situation.

"That was no luck," a voice called to me. It was Chelsea speaking. She was staring at me with large brown eyes. "Reed, right? That was skill, and I hear you have it in spades."

Someone snorted behind me and I could tell it was Delphine. Blood rushed to my face. I was embarrassed by Chelsea's praise. Wait, she already knew who I was? I was confused, but flattered that she was calling me out among everyone.

"Well, let's give Marcus a fair shot," Ames said. "Time to go at it once more," he ordered, directing us to the center area again.

I bent down prepared to take on Marcus again, and got into a wrestling stance. He finally made eye contact with me, and I could see he was furious.

We circled around each other, waiting for the other person to make the first move.

All of a sudden, Marcus charged my direction and wrapped his arms around me to try to throw me to the ground. I was substantially bigger than him, and staggered back a few steps, but didn't fall. I shook him off and we reset, both appraising the situation.

"Go for his knees," Benny yelled to Marcus,

and I glared at him. In the split second that I stopped to look at Benny, Marcus lunged at me again and took me out at the shins.

He was small, but he was able to knock me off my feet. My body flung backwards and I heard everyone yell out, their screams echoing around in my head. It must have been a pretty spectacular fall. My head smacked hard into the ground and everything went black.

CHAPTER 14

When I woke up, the first thing I saw was a woman, older than Chelsea, with long, dark hair staring down at me. There was a fluorescent light hanging from a cord, swaying slowly back and forth above her head. I seemed to be in a doctor's examination room of some sort. Metal instruments and gauze were strewn across a stainless steel counter behind her.

She stared at me with brows furrowed and bent down to shine a light in my pupils.

"How are you feeling?" she asked.

"Awful." I mumbled. My head was throbbing and I felt a sharp pain emanating out the back.

"Here, take this," she said, shoving a few pills into my lips as she held up a little cup of water to my mouth. "Lift up your head," she instructed.

I hesitated and contemplated spitting them out. "Are you drugging me?"

"It's ibuprofen, don't worry," she assured. I was in too much pain to argue further, and weakly swallowed the pills.

"You got a pretty nasty bump on the back of your head. You landed right on a rock sticking out of the ground over there. What are the chances?" she asked, and I groaned.

She dabbed at my forehead with a cool cloth. "This nasty little injury might delay your debut," she said. Then, she continued, muttering under her breath, "Gareth wouldn't like that one bit." I wasn't sure if she was talking to herself or to me.

"My debut? What do you mean?" I asked.

"Oh sweetie, you don't know, do you?" she said, looking at me like I was pitiful.

"What? I don't understand. Who's Gareth anyway? No one is telling us anything," I said.

"Now, look, I've gotten you all worked up when you really need to rest. You'll learn more soon enough," she said as she pushed gently on my shoulders, forcing me to recline back again.

"Is this part of the program too?" I asked, feeling disoriented. What was this place?

"What program?"

She seemed confused by my question.

"Ship Out," I said, trying to read her expression.

She laughed to herself. "Oh, honey," she said, shaking her head. "What have they done?" she said under her breath.

"What do you mean?"

"Let's talk about something else. I'm lonely. They don't let me out much," she said. "My name's Elise," she smiled down at me. "Would you like some food? I can get you a dinner just like the ones you've been treated to in the training camp."

I nodded. I was famished.

"Okay then, be back in a few," she said and then left the room. As soon as she exited, I heard a latch lock on the door.

Despite feeling terrible, I stood up and held onto the counter to catch myself from falling. I opened all the cabinet doors, searching for hints as to where I was, or how I could escape. It seemed like an ordinary examination room at a doctor's office, but there was no scale, no magazines, or anything else. The metal instruments, gauze, and bottles filled with mysterious liquids were the only things on the counters and in the cabinets. The bottles were all etched with an ornate P symbol, the same one from the boat, and I wondered what it stood for.

Elise came back carrying a steaming-hot chicken pot pie on a tray.

"So, where are you from?" she asked, placing the tray in front of me.

"Oregon," I said.

"Oh, I remember Oregon," she responded, staring off at the wall behind me.

"Where are you from?" I asked her as I took a bite of food, hoping to get more clues about who she was and where we were.

"Well, I've been here—on the island, that is— for a very long time. I'm a native, you could say," she said.

"And where are we?" I asked, wanting to know what this place was.

"Hidden away, Reed. It doesn't matter where, really, as up until now, we can't be found."

I looked at her, not understanding.

She continued, "Anyway, I've already said too much. That's a problem for me, unfortunately. I have a big mouth. I think I should call it a night before I get us both in trouble," she said as she pulled the blanket over me, and gently touched my forehead with her palm.

"Goodnight, Reed. I will see you in the

morning," she said. She got up and was gone before I could ask anything more.

Even though there was no clock or windows in the room, I guessed it was very late. My mind raced as I tried to piece together what was happening. I was certain this wasn't part of the Ship Out program any longer, and I felt uneasy.

It was pitch black and I lay on the hard, narrow bed, trying to figure out my next step. All of a sudden, the door creaked open and a sliver of light filled the room.

A silhouette of a girl appeared in the frame and the door quickly shut again, returning the room to darkness.

I heard someone stumble toward my bed, and then sit down on the edge next to me.

"Who is it?" I asked, feeling scared.

"Shhh . . . it's Chelsea," the person hissed.

"What? Why are you here?"

"I'm not supposed to be, so keep it down. I

wanted to see if you were okay," she said, and I suddenly felt her hand resting on my arm.

My heartbeat quickened and I could tell I was blushing. I was thankful she couldn't see me.

"That was quite a showing today. But you gave everyone a scare. You are a much better fighter than Marcus," she said. "You're going to be popular, I can tell."

"With who?" I asked.

"I'd rather not say too much as I'm not sure if I can trust you yet. But, I want to give you some advice," she said. I was quiet, waiting to hear what she was going to say.

"When it's your turn to fight, you cannot hesitate."

"What are you talking about?"

She ignored me, continuing, "It'll be unnatural and you won't want to take action, but you must fight with no pause in your head or your heart if you want to make it here," she said, and then grew quiet. I strained to see her in the darkness. I didn't understand what she was saying.

"But, also remember they want a good show. Actually, it's demanded of you here," she said firmly, squeezing my forearm.

"What do you mean?" I asked. I was confused why both Elise and Chelsea couldn't—or chose not to—share any more with me.

At that moment, there was a loud shuffling sound overhead. It sounded like people were walking down a hallway.

"I gotta go," Chelsea said. She reached down and kissed me lightly on the forehead, her hair brushing against my cheeks. I felt my face turn hot.

"Be careful," she warned as she opened the door and was gone again before I knew it.

I sat in bed the rest of the night, tossing and turning. When it was morning, Elise came in with a pot of coffee and a plate of eggs, bacon, and toast.

"How did you sleep?" she asked.

"Terribly," I admitted. I didn't want to get Chelsea in trouble, so I didn't say anything about her visit.

I ate in silence, but couldn't resist asking a question. I tried to sound casual. "So, who's Chelsea?"

Elise looked at me and smirked with a knowing expression. "Why are you asking about her?"

"She was at our training session yesterday," I said, maybe too quickly.

"You have a crush, don't you?" she asked and gazed at me with a smirk.

"No, I'm just trying to learn more about where the hell I am right now and who you people are," I said, lying.

"Don't worry. Everyone fancies Chelsea. She is beautiful, isn't she?" Elise spoke, looking me directly in the eye.

"Yes, that's hard to argue."

"Just so you know, you're barking up the wrong

tree with that one. Now turn around so I can look at that head," she ordered as she gently twisted me around to look at my wound.

After examining it and re-applying a new bandage, Elise declared that I was fine to go back to training, but that I had to take it easy. "Let's go," she said, grabbing me by the arm.

"Oh, and I almost forgot," she said as she plucked the gauze roll from the counter and wrapped a long strand around my eyes several times, obstructing my view. I winced from the gauze being pulled tight against my wound. "This will have to do." It was a haphazard blindfold, but it did the trick. As I stumbled forward, Elise grabbed me by the arm to guide me.

She led me out the door and I couldn't see at first. But, as we walked, my blindfold loosened and I started to be able to peek through the gauze just a tiny bit. We shuffled slowly through what seemed to be an outdoor corridor built out of tall columns of white marble and marble tiles on the ground. Occasionally, I glimpsed groups of women huddled in the hallways—I caught bare shoulders and manicured feet. I also heard hushed voices and giggles when I passed.

"Shhh!" Elise hissed at each group, and I wondered who these women were. I considered calling out to them for help, but didn't want to draw attention to the fact that I could see out of Elise's messy blindfold.

It was a long walk, and I also caught sight of half-dressed men of varying degrees of fitness—some were young and buff, while others appeared flabby and hairy and out of shape. Elise giggled and said "hi" in a flirty voice when we passed each group of men.

"Who are you talking to?" I asked as she walked briskly, pulling at my arm and causing me to stumble over my own feet.

"You should mind your business, Reed," she warned. "Now, we're almost there."

Just then, I heard a distant cheering, like a

crowd watching a sporting match. The cheers got louder as we walked. I looked in the direction of the noise, tipping my head upwards to try to peek through holes in the gauze better. "What is that?" I asked.

Elise wouldn't say another word to me and she dragged me along quicker. She turned back and caught my eyes through the gaps in the gauze.

"Oh Reed, why didn't you say something? You could get in very big trouble," she warned, as she quickly retied the gauze firmly and I was sightless once again.

Finally, after walking several more minutes, she took off my blindfold and I was in the center area of our living quarters. Everyone was still in their beds, and several people stirred when they heard me enter.

Elise led me to my cell and locked the door behind me. Marcus grimaced and glanced away.

Carl, stationed in the next cell, came over to the bars closest to where I was standing. "Dude, are you okay?" he asked. "We've all been worried about you," he said.

"I'm fine. Glad to be back."

"Man, you took a good hit. How you feelin'?" Micah asked.

"Sore." This was an understatement, but I didn't want to talk about my injury. Rather, I was thinking about what Elise and Chelsea shared with me. This wasn't the forum to tell Micah what they said—with everyone listening and watching us. But I was eager to take him aside to talk about it and get his thoughts.

I locked eyes with Delphine and she appeared concerned, but then she looked away. I felt like I had disappointed her in some way, but I couldn't put my finger on it.

Just then, Darby entered the room. "Rise and shine, friends. Reed, glad to see you back. You'll be sitting on the sidelines for now, but I want you to still come and watch practice today, okay?"

I nodded. Whatever Darby said, I was going to do. What choice did I have?

Everyone got dressed and we headed out to the courtyard area.

Chelsea was already there, again sitting in the purple chair, looking casual and well rested. She glanced at me and I smiled back, searching for any hints of recognition on her face about our encounter last night.

Delphine moved forward and stood next to me, grabbing my arm and squeezing it. It felt like she was marking her territory. I pulled away. She looked at me, surprised, and then stepped off to join Micah, who was standing on the other side of the group. I could feel her glare at me.

Just then, Ames and Max came outside, each carrying a large bin filled with wooden swords, spears, and other instruments.

"Now we get down to serious business," Ames explained, pulling out one of the long wooden swords. I could see they had rounded tips. "These are child's play, but you have to learn how to crawl before you can run," he explained.

He handed everyone a sword or a spear except me as I was ordered to rest for the day. As I stood by and watched, everybody practiced swinging and thrusting the instruments up, out, and downward.

"It's not the real thing, of course, but you have to start somewhere," he said.

"Why are we doing this again?" Micah asked.

"Fortitude of mind, body, and spirit," Darby said, standing next to Chelsea, who nodded her head.

As the group trained, everyone joked around, but I remained quiet. I remembered both Elise and Chelsea's words and I wondered what was really happening here.

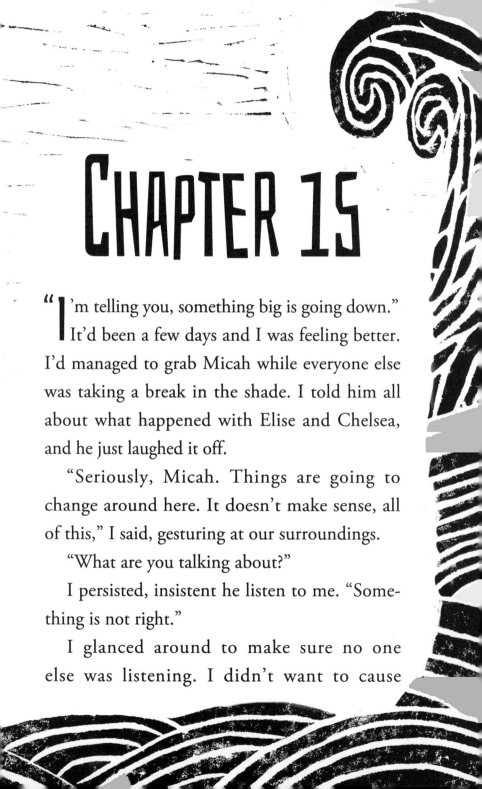

CHAPTER 15

"I'm telling you, something big is going down." It'd been a few days and I was feeling better. I'd managed to grab Micah while everyone else was taking a break in the shade. I told him all about what happened with Elise and Chelsea, and he just laughed it off.

"Seriously, Micah. Things are going to change around here. It doesn't make sense, all of this," I said, gesturing at our surroundings.

"What are you talking about?"

I persisted, insistent he listen to me. "Something is not right."

I glanced around to make sure no one else was listening. I didn't want to cause unnecessary alarm among the group, and Micah was the obvious person to talk to about this. For some reason, I felt like he'd know what to do.

"Yeah, a week or so to go and then we get to head home," he said. "I can't wait to return to my parents, even if they're assholes. But they're *my* assholes."

"Speaking of heading home," I interjected, as something had been bothering me a lot. "I've been thinking—we must get on an airplane, right? It would take too long to sail back."

Micah stared at me blankly, like he didn't understand. If I was calculating everything correctly, we had been gone almost three months now and we were supposed to be home at the end of August. There was no way we could sail back in time. I finally blurted out what I was really getting at.

"We're not on the program any longer, Micah," I said.

He raised his eyebrows.

"What do you mean?"

"That's what I've been trying to tell you. I think this place is something much worse than Ship Out. The training and jail cells are weird, right? And why haven't we seen Titus, True, or Sully since arriving?" I asked, pushing the issue.

"I don't know, man. That doesn't make any sense, either. If it's not part of Ship Out, what is this place?" he asked, shrugging. "And why are we here?"

"I'm not sure, but I think we might have to fight, and that's why we're training so hard," I said, trying to get him to come around and believe me so we could work on an escape plan together.

"If that's true, who are we going to fight?" he asked.

"I have no idea. Maybe this is some sort of military training?" I guessed.

Micah seemed unsure, so I continued talking.

"Anyway, that doctor Elise told me I wouldn't be ready for my debut, and Chelsea said—"

"Yeah, go back to Chelsea for a second. You're telling me she came in to see you in the middle of the night? Are you sure?" he laughed, but looked at me, concerned.

"Positive."

"Nah, maybe Elise *did* drug you!" he joked.

"I swear. Chelsea was sitting right next to me, touching me."

"Okay. Now you're getting somewhere—" Micah joked before we were interrupted.

"What are you guys talking about?"

It was Delphine. She was standing right behind us.

"After Reed's head injury, he said Chelsea visited him in the middle of the night, but I think Elise must've drugged him," Micah said.

I shot him an annoyed look.

"What?" Delphine asked. "Who's Elise? The doctor? And what's up with Chelsea? She seems terrible."

"Oh, it's nothing," I said, wanting to change

the subject. "She's alright—" I felt like I needed to defend Chelsea, but I wasn't sure why.

"Who is that girl anyway? Why is she here?" Delphine asked.

"I have no idea," I admitted. "But I think something bad is going on here. When Elise led me back to our living quarters, I saw some weird things," I said and glanced around to see if anyone was listening. Everyone else was sprawled on the ground, out of earshot.

"Oh yeah? Like what?" Delphine asked, perking up. Micah leaned in as well.

"Well, I was supposed to have a blindfold on, but it was falling off and I saw other people milling about. And, none of them were wearing much clothing."

"You're losing it. I'm starting to get worried about you. Are you sure?" Micah asked.

"And I heard loud cheering in the distance. Like at a football game."

"So, if what you're saying is true, what do you think it all means?" Micah asked.

Just then, Ames yelled across the courtyard, and we couldn't discuss it any more. "Time to get back at it," he ordered.

"We can talk more about this tomorrow, okay? We need to come up with a way out of here," I said as we walked back to the group.

"Okay, man," Micah said, but he sounded unsure.

Ames and Max proceeded to pair us off, and stuck me with Delphine. I glanced at her and she stuck her tongue out at me.

Ames stood before us, while Max handed each of us a small wooden dagger.

"You'll see that I've put you against someone who seems like a mismatch on the surface. Like Reed and Delphine for example," he nodded at us.

"Hey, I take offense to that!" Delphine chimed in.

"Delphine. I mean this as a compliment.

Because it just appears like a mismatch. You're small, but very tough," Ames said.

She smiled and shook her head yes.

"Okay, well, let's prove this theory out. Everyone, time to engage in lightning sparring rounds with your partner."

He then turned to Max. "Okay, you can let Gareth know we're ready."

Max spoke a message into his wristlet. As he did that, Ames ordered us to spread out across the courtyard.

A man suddenly came through the door, flanked by two of the White Suits and Darby. He was distinguished-looking, with thick salt-and-pepper hair and tanned skin. He sat in one of the purple chairs. Darby sat beside him, and the other two men stood just behind them.

We all stopped and looked at the men. So, this was Gareth.

"Carry on," Darby said.

"Yes, don't mind Gareth, he's just here to

observe," Ames instructed. We continued with practice, and I knew we were supposed to impress Gareth, but I wasn't sure why exactly.

"You ready?" Delphine asked with a grin on her face.

"Yeah, show me what you got," I said. Without hesitation, Delphine charged forward gracefully and swung out her dagger tapping me firmly in the stomach.

"If that had been real, you'd be dead," Ames said. "Try a bit harder, Reed," he instructed.

We reset and I swung out at Delphine, who smiled as she easily blocked my strike with her dagger, and then counter-swung again, hitting me this time in the heart.

I stumbled back and looked at Delphine, surprised. She shrugged like it was no big deal, and laughed.

"Come on, Reed, I know you can give me better than that," she taunted.

I saw behind her that Gareth and Darby were

whispering to each other in their chairs, watching us spar.

Chelsea's words about not hesitating came to me again. This must be the test she was warning me about, I realized.

"Okay, you asked for it," I said, and lunged in Delphine's direction, taking her down in one fell swoop to the grass. We landed hard with a thud and I was now straddling her. She stared up at me wide-eyed and smiled.

"Not so fast," she said and punched her dagger at my chest, causing me to fall back, allowing her to scramble out from underneath me. She rolled away and quickly stood up, then stabbed the wooden weapon at me once again.

"Bravo! Bravo!" Gareth stood up, clapping his hands. Everyone around us stopped fighting for a moment and looked over at him.

"Delphine, is it?" he asked, and she nodded. "Come on over here. I'd like to shake your hand," he said.

Delphine walked over and reached out her arm. Gareth took it with his right hand, and then put his left hand firmly over their handshake. He locked eyes with her and smiled.

"You've impressed me. I like what I see," he said.

"Thank you," Delphine responded and after a long pause, pulled her hand away.

"And you, Reed," he called to me. "I've heard you're good as well, but you let Delphine walk all over you."

He gazed at me with disdain and I felt like an idiot.

"I'll expect better the next time we meet," he said to me. He then proceeded to call out observations about the other kids in our group to Ames and Max.

"Benny isn't strong enough yet. Neither is Trevor." Ames agreed, and then Gareth kept rattling off his thoughts about all of us. We stood there unmoving, listening to his critique. "Marcus looks mean—which you know I like. But, he's not ready yet, either. Carl is a tough one, isn't he? Micah looks the part . . . Rose has potential, but she needs some thorns—work on that—" he kept on going, telling Ames and Max things about us that he wanted them to change.

While he was talking, Delphine came and stood next to me. She whispered "sorry," but she was smiling wide.

As we headed back to the living quarters at the end of the day, Micah walked alongside me.

"What was that about?" he asked.

"Maybe it was our debut—the thing Elise warned me about?" I said, shrugging, but that didn't seem right.

That night, as we ate our dinner, everyone compared notes about the best way to swing a dagger, or how to dart out the way of an opponent that was bigger.

I could tell everybody felt safe, so it was easier

not to question too much what was happening. Our trip was almost over, right?

Delphine sat next to me at the table. She leaned in and put her head on my shoulder. As we sat there, I couldn't help but think about Chelsea, and her warm body sitting next to me on the bed in the darkness.

CHAPTER 16

I was having the same dream I had every couple of months—it was me and James wrestling in our backyard. I was in the grass and he was on top of me, pinning me down and laughing. The sun shone above us, obscuring his face, but in the dream, his laughter rang out clear as a bell.

As he held me down, I also heard my dad cheering, and when I turned my head to look at my dad, James suddenly wasn't there anymore. His weight upon me disappeared, and when I glanced back, all I saw was the sun. It was at that moment, every time I had the dream, I'd wake up with a start.

Sure enough, this time I jolted upright in bed and Marcus was looking at me from his cot.

"Someone's here for you," he said, nodding toward the center area.

"What?" I was still half asleep.

"Over there. Darby is asking for you and Carl," he said.

I turned my head and Darby plus two White Suits were standing just outside my cell.

"Glad we didn't have to wake you up," Darby said. "You okay? You look like you just saw a ghost."

"Yeah, I'm fine . . . wait . . . what time is it?" I asked, as I looked around. The room was still dim and everyone else was asleep. I saw Carl across the room getting dressed quietly.

"It's early. We need you to get ready and come with us," Darby said.

"Just me?" I asked, trying not to sound worried.

"Just you and Carl, for now," he said.

"Why?"

"You'll see, my friend," he said. "Now come on."

I quickly got dressed in sweatpants and a t-shirt, and slid out of the cell door, which a White Suit was holding open. As I was leaving, I looked back at Marcus one last time.

"Have fun," he said, and then lay back down and rolled over, putting the pillow over his head.

We moved toward Carl's cell and he soon stood next to me, also appearing nervous. I had no idea why they were singling out just the two of us, or where we were going.

Maybe my parents were here? Maybe they finally had a change of heart and were coming to take me home a little bit early?

If anyone had the means to do that, it would be my dad. I didn't *really* believe it, but the thought crossed my mind for a split second.

As we walked down the dark hallway that led to the training area, Carl glanced over at me.

"Do you know where we're going?" he asked.

"No idea," I responded and Carl seemed scared.

"It'll be okay man. Let's just stick together, okay?" I said.

He nodded. "Of course."

Darby led us to a new hallway that we hadn't been to yet.

At the end of that hall, I saw two dimly lit gold doors, one on the left and the other on the right.

He then turned to us. "Okay, guys, time to separate. Reed, go in the door on the left and Carl, you head into the one on the right," he ordered, and as if on cue, the doors cracked open slightly, but we couldn't see who was on the other side.

"What's going on, Darby?" I asked again.

"Your fate is what it is. Now go in and get ready. And listen to what your guides tell you, okay?" he said, and wouldn't offer up any more, instead nudging us each toward separate doors. I looked at Carl and we made eye contact for a second.

"It's okay man," I felt compelled to say, but had no idea if that was true.

"I know," he responded before disappearing through the door on the right, which shut quickly behind him.

Darby then nudged me in the shoulder, and I knew I had no choice but to walk into the room. When I went inside, I was surprised to see Ames standing there, waiting for me. He closed the door behind me.

Inside the dark room I saw two armchairs and a large metal closet with a lock on it. The area was only lit by torches on the white marble walls.

"Okay, time to get dressed and rest up until we're called upstairs," Ames said.

"Called upstairs? What do you mean? What is this place?" My legs felt like they were going to buckle beneath me. He took a pair of small white shorts out of the closet and ordered that I put them on. I was sick to my stomach. The door opened and a woman came in carrying a small case.

"Who's this?" I asked Ames.

"She's here to put the finishing touches on your look. It's what the crowd likes," he said.

"What crowd?" I asked. He didn't respond, but the woman came over and without speaking, opened her case and revealed it was filled with what appeared to be different color paints. As Ames watched, she proceeded to paint my body in bright colors—red, blue, yellow—and put streaks across my cheeks. The liquid was cold and I squirmed, but I knew there was nowhere for me to escape to and so I just stood there, feeling terrified and humiliated. Then, when she was done painting, the woman taped a small microphone just above my heart.

"What's this for?" I asked, but neither answered.

When the woman was done, Ames approved, and she left the room.

"What is this place?" I asked.

"Sit down," Ames ordered and we walked over to the armchairs and I rested gingerly at the edge of one of the chairs, too nervous to relax. He sat across from me and leaned in close, talking very quietly.

"Listen. I'm not supposed to tell you anything, Reed. But, honestly, I think you may be able to help me one day. And I trust that if you make it out, you'll keep what I share a secret. You understand?" he asked, dead serious. "I'll get killed if you talk to anyone. Gareth will know," he said, looking me straight in the eye. "You got me?"

"Yes. Okay."

He sighed deeply and there was a long pause before he began talking again.

"You're at Gladiator Island, Reed. Well, at least that's what we staff call it. To visitors, it's actually Praeclarus Island," he said.

"What's that?" I asked.

"Have you heard the name Gareth Conway before?" he asked. I shook my head.

"Your dad knows him, and if we can get to him, your dad is the one that can help get us out of here," he said and I snapped upright, surprised Ames knew who my dad was too.

"What does my dad have to do with anything? I'm confused."

"Gareth was also an internet tycoon, but he went off the grid nearly twenty years ago. Faked a plane crash so he could 'retire' from his life and work on his passion project—this island and running Praeclarus," he explained.

"What's Praeclarus? Where are we?" I asked, totally confused.

"Well, even I don't know where we are exactly."

"But, what is this place? What is Praeclarus? And what does my dad have to do with it?"

He hesitated. "I'm trusting you, Reed," He seemed to say it mostly to himself, and then sighed.

"I won't tell anyone—"

"Well, this island is a billionaire's playground.

It's the one place the ultra-rich and ultra-famous can come to explore all their basest, ugliest desires. It's a very, very exclusive club. Whatever they fancy, Gareth makes it a reality here. He prides himself on it, actually."

"Like what?"

"Women. Men. Drugs. You name it. But that stuff bores Gareth a bit these days. His real interest is what you'll see upstairs," Ames said.

"What's upstairs?" I asked, feeling scared. "And how can my dad help?"

"We'll have to talk about that later. You're going to be called out any minute."

Ames got up from the chair and took a key hanging from a chain on his neck to open the metal cabinet. He pulled out a long, shiny dagger lined with rubies in its handle. He carried it on both hands, palms up.

"Go ahead, take it," he commanded. "You have to get used to the weight in your hand," he said. I reached out and gingerly picked it up by the jeweled handle. It was heavier than it looked, especially when compared to the plain wooden swords we'd been practicing with.

"What's this for?" I asked, looking up at him, feeling scared.

"I think you know exactly what that's for, Reed," Ames said, holding both of my shoulders firmly.

I didn't want to believe it. This couldn't be real.

I wanted nothing more than for my parents to walk through the door, and for my dad to say, *"Gotcha! You're scared shitless, huh? Promise to start acting like a real man? Yes? Well, then, let's get out of here and head back home."*

I saw the image flash through my mind, but no one opened the door.

"You expect me to actually use this?" I asked, not believing this was actually happening.

"If you're going to survive, you *have* to use it," he said, looking me straight in the eye.

"I can't," I said, shaking my head. "Against Carl?"

Ames stared at me long and hard. "Let me say it again. If you're going to make it out of here alive, you *have* to use it."

Just then, Ames's wristlet buzzed and a voice asked, "Are you ready?" Ames said yes.

"This is what I've been training you for, Reed," Ames said. "You have the tools you need to come out a victor. Carl is fast, but much smaller than you. Use your strength and your brain, okay?" He looked at me and I nodded. Just then, his wristlet buzzed again.

"Time to go."

Ames led me down the hallway we had been in earlier. We came to a very large metal gate. It was probably twenty feet tall.

"When you get out there, don't look scared, okay?" Ames said. "They'll see that immediately. They like strong fighters."

"Who are *they*?" I asked desperately as he turned on the mic on my chest.

"No more time to talk, Reed." Ames said, moving over to the gate and entering a code. The gate rose slowly and I was blinded by sunlight and the eruption of a frenzied crowd.

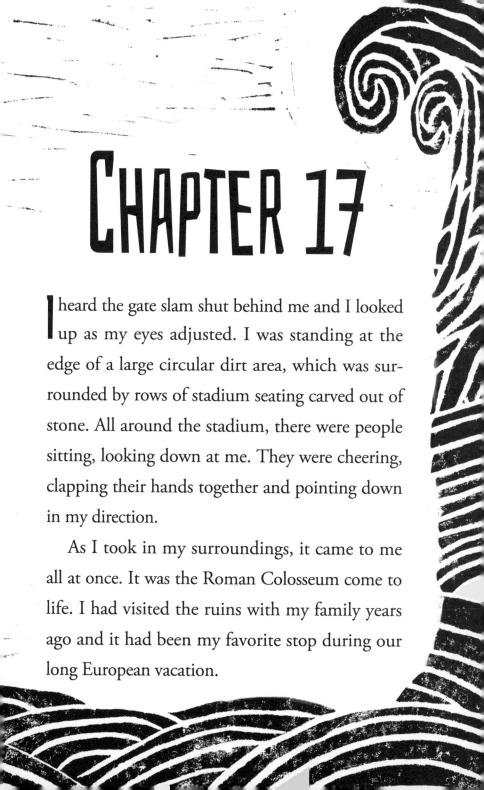

CHAPTER 17

I heard the gate slam shut behind me and I looked up as my eyes adjusted. I was standing at the edge of a large circular dirt area, which was surrounded by rows of stadium seating carved out of stone. All around the stadium, there were people sitting, looking down at me. They were cheering, clapping their hands together and pointing down in my direction.

As I took in my surroundings, it came to me all at once. It was the Roman Colosseum come to life. I had visited the ruins with my family years ago and it had been my favorite stop during our long European vacation.

I'm standing in a coliseum, and I'm the fighter here to entertain.

All the cryptic words from Elise, Chelsea, and Ames were starting to make sense. I looked around for Carl, but didn't see him anywhere.

Just then, two of the White Suits came over and lifted me up by my armpits, dragging me to the other side of the Coliseum floor.

"I'm not doing this!" I yelled out, trying to pull away from their grip. I contemplated stabbing them with my dagger, but looking around, saw that I was outnumbered by Suits who could easily take me out. The men and women in the stands went crazy, laughing and screaming in English and other languages I didn't recognize.

I looked up to an area of the stands where a squadron of White Suits was flanking a couple of rows. In the center, there were two tall, gold thrones draped with purple velvet fabric. In one chair sat Gareth, pleased and relaxed. He was clapping heartily, looking down at me. And then, in the chair next to him sat Chelsea, her mouth open in laughter.

"What are you doing there?" I yelled up to her, but my words were drowned out by the crowd.

The wall separating us was at least ten feet tall. As I spotted Chelsea, I saw someone behind her who looked familiar. He was wearing a white suit, the hat and sunglasses, but I was almost certain it was Titus.

Before I had time to process that connection, I heard the gate creak open again. I swung around to see Carl walking through it, appearing bewildered. He was holding what looked like a long wooden spear with a sharp metal point, tightly gripped in his left hand. A spear vs. a dagger? That hardly seemed fair.

Two of the Suits flanked him on each side, and pulled him over to us. They dropped him next to me.

Despite his obvious fear, he was a sight to behold, tanned and muscular, the paint accenting his stomach muscles. I couldn't help but feel intimidated for a moment, knowing what we were about to face.

"Where are we?" Carl yelled out, and I couldn't tell if he was directing the question to me, up at Gareth, or up to the skies, cursing his lot to be in this situation.

I glanced around at the stands and estimated there were about two hundred people in total looking down at us, waiting. Who were these people? Where did they come from, and how did they get here?

They were mostly men, with a few women peppered throughout. I saw some attractive women in gauzy clothing leaning next to fat, ugly men, putting their arms lazily around shoulders or nuzzling necks. Many of the people were wearing white suits and I gathered they were employees at the island.

I then turned my head back toward Gareth and Chelsea. I wondered why she was there. Was

Gareth forcing her to be his lover? She was probably too scared to call out to me.

I was determined to figure out a way to save her from this place. We'd get out of here together. The fantasy flashed before me for just an instant.

I remembered how Ames said that he needed me, and I wondered how we could get to my dad. I saw Ames now seated directly behind Gareth, and he looked down at me, conveying no hint of the conversations we'd had.

Two White Suits were standing between me and Carl, at the ready, holding something in their hands. I glanced down and saw it was the same type of instrument that Titus had used against me on the boat when he zapped me.

So many questions raced through my mind as the shouts above me got louder and louder.

I didn't want to give them what they wanted, and I quickly searched for a way out, but there was none to be had. Could I talk myself out of this?

"Gareth!" I yelled up to him, and he peered down at me with curiosity.

"Yes, Reed?" He asked, shushing the crowd so he could hear.

"Are you making us fight each other? You can't do this to us. It's illegal," I screamed, and the words sounded silly as they came out of my mouth.

Gareth laughed heartily, and I heard men and women cackling above me, then Chelsea. I glared at her, surprised that she'd give him the satisfaction of laughing at me. She disregarded my look and tossed her hair back, giggling.

A big screen on the far end of the Coliseum projected Chelsea's perfect smile in close up, the crowd audibly oohed and gave catcalls in her direction.

As I was standing there, my parents flashed into my mind and I thought about dying here. It suddenly felt inevitable, as I looked over at the long spear Carl was holding.

I wondered if my parents knew our boat was missing, and if they were searching for me. Maybe they just assumed they hadn't heard from the boat or me for weeks because of the Ship Out program rules. It would probably be another week before they realized something was amiss when we didn't return home.

And then, a terrible thought crossed my mind—did Gareth seek me out specifically? Did he really know my dad, like Ames said? They *must've* known each other, given their occupations and success, right?

And if that were true, how did Gareth find me, and what about the other kids on the boat? It didn't make sense.

I sat down on the dirt, gingerly holding onto the dagger for fear of putting it down, and boos erupted around me. Something hit my head with a painful thunk, and I glanced down to see a large rock lying next to me. "Get up!" people yelled.

Gareth, unamused, motioned to the Suits and they pulled me off the ground, and held me there.

Carl looked at me. "Man, what's happening?" he yelled.

I remembered Ames's words about appearing strong, and forced myself to stand upright and glared at Gareth, who stood up to address the crowd.

Everyone became quiet again, anxiously awaiting what he was about to say. Chelsea stared up at him with adoration.

"Hello again, my Praeclarus friends!" Gareth boomed out, his voice carrying through the stadium's speakers and his tanned face beaming on the jumbo screen. The cheers were frenzied. The men and women that had gathered were excited to hear him speak. I could tell he wielded power over them.

Chelsea stood up as well and put her arm around Gareth, waving at the crowd. She was like a shooting star that everyone strained to glimpse, and just her appearance sent everyone into a frenzy.

"Okay, okay," Gareth continued, waiting for everyone to finally quiet down. "Welcome my friends to a very special day. We have a new batch of recruits on the island, and I have to say, they are a promising bunch. I've picked Carl—the blond—for this first fight because he's an aggressive one, and I think you'll be surprised that his small size is misleading. And Reed, the tall one—we all know why he's special," he said.

What did that mean?

Gareth continued, "But, he's also a promising fighter, which is surprising to me." I heard men and women laughing. "We all remember the rules, right? We'll give them a chance to fight on their own, and if needed, I'll provide a prompt," he said, and just then, the gate rose again and four new White Suits walked through, each carrying a bow, arrows, and a bucket.

The gate closed behind them, and they each

walked to a corner of the stadium. Carl and I looked around at them, and I wondered what was happening, exactly. Were they going to shoot us?

Gareth continued to speak. "And remember, ten wins and these boys get a new life," he said and the screen showed a close-up of his face, grinning with eyebrows raised. "Other than that, there are no rules, just how you like it."

After Gareth was done speaking, the Suits guarding us pulled Carl and I away from each other, so that we were in the center of the stadium, about thirty yards apart. Carl stood with the long spear raised by his side. Even at that distance, I saw that his arm was trembling.

I screamed out to Carl, "Dude, this isn't real! It can't be! We can get out of this together!"

"You're right! I won't do anything if you won't!" Carl yelled and we just stood there, each refusing to move forward. People were throwing rocks, bottles, and food down at us, but we stood still, and I felt a connection to Carl that we'd both remain firm and unyielding. *Put us in solitary confinement, I don't care*, I thought.

"Let them lock us up!" I called to him.

"Sigh. I had a feeling this would happen, newbies and all," Gareth said, sounding disappointed. "Shooters, you may proceed," he ordered and I saw one of the White Suits in the corner dip an arrow into his bucket. He then pulled something out of his pocket—I couldn't see what it was. But, when he put it against the arrow he was holding, the tip suddenly lit up, engulfed in flames.

"What's that?" Carl screamed out, and he pivoted, looking around. I followed his eyes as he turned, and saw that all four Suits in the corners were now holding flaming arrows, pulling them taut and aiming them at us.

The audience kept on throwing rocks and bottles, and I felt a stone hit me hard in the back, but I refused to move forward. Carl appeared more and more agitated. Suddenly, I saw an arrow coming toward me and I jumped to the left quickly, letting the fiery stick zip past and land on the dirt floor just behind me.

"What the hell?" I screamed out, not sure what to do. I had nowhere to escape.

Then, an arrow shot toward Carl, and it hit his painted left calf, which lit up in flames quickly. He screamed and fell to the ground, rolling around frantically until the fire was snuffed out.

"Are you okay?" I yelled, and to my surprise, instead of responding, Carl suddenly jumped up, looking angry. He began to charge forward, first jogging, then sprinting toward me. As Carl got within striking distance, I opened my mouth, searching for the words to stop him. To my horror, Carl thrust his spear in my direction, and I dove out of the way just as the blade pierced my skin.

A dizzying pain shot through my shoulder and I stumbled and fell hard on my back into the dirt, dropping my own weapon. I howled loudly and glanced at the blood pouring down my chest. I looked up in disbelief at Carl, who stood holding the spear that was still lodged in the fleshy area between my shoulder and chest. He appeared terrified and uncertain what to do next. I grabbed the rod of the spear with both hands and yanked the tip out, gasping from the pain. This wrenched the handle out of Carl's grip and he lunged at me again.

As if by instinct, I swung the spear at him. The wooden pole cracked into the side of his head, breaking in two. The blow ripped open his ear and sent him stumbling backwards. Carl grabbed at his head and screamed.

I watched as blood pooled in Carl's ear and dripped down his face onto the dirt. He grabbed the wooden shard of the half-spear and ran toward me. I quickly rolled away and hopped up to my feet.

Friends just hours before; I couldn't believe how quickly the situation had turned. *This is actually happening*, I thought. *Carl is trying to kill me.*

Out of the corner of my eye, I saw the screen project a giant image of Chelsea smiling down at me, and leaning into Gareth to laugh.

I quickly scanned the arena floor, looking for my weapon and trying to find any way to escape. The gate I had been led out of had since been closed and locked shut and there were Suits stationed everywhere.

At that moment, I felt sick. I finally understood—without a doubt—that the only escape from the situation was to kill Carl. *Carl had obviously come to this truth more quickly*, I thought, *and was doing what was necessary to get out of here alive.* I needed to catch up quickly.

Carl set his legs in a lunge, like he was about to charge at me again. He was preparing to plunge the sharp wooden shank of the spear handle into my heart. Remembering Ames' words about survival at any cost, I snatched the other half-spear, the one with the tip, from the ground.

I moved toward Carl and flung the spear

toward his chest. He lost his balance trying to pivot out of the way, but my weapon missed him. He resumed his charge and jabbed his wooden stick's jagged edge into my thigh, causing me to scream out in pain. I knew I couldn't stop to think about the injury, so I lunged to the side and grabbed my discarded dagger from the ground and jumped on top of him, weapon in hand. Carl tried to twist out from under my weight but couldn't wriggle free. He swung his arms upward and grabbed hold of my neck, trying to push me away.

I gasped for air and brought the dagger up over my head, about to strike. "Reed! Please don't!" Carl pleaded, even as he gripped my neck in one last desperate move to overtake me. I closed my eyes tightly, and stabbed downward, the weapon's sharp tip slicing more easily than I expected into Carl's chest.

Carl's mouth opened wide to scream. He grabbed at the blade lodged in his body. I wrenched it out quickly and raised the dagger again, delivering a second blow. Carl's cries were quieted first by the jeers and applause, then by the blood coming up from his throat and choking him.

Carl struggled beneath me, the bloody metal blade still protruding from his chest. His breathing was labored and slow now, and his gaze was bright with pain. He was still alive, which seemed crueler to me than death at this point. I wondered how long it would take. I contemplated my next move and realized Gareth and the people cheering wanted the struggle to last as long as possible. I couldn't bear watching Carl gasp for his last breaths, so I pulled the weapon out of his chest. Carl whimpered for a moment, then went quiet.

I plunged the dripping tip into his heart, feeling his blood spray my face, and Carl's body went limp moments later. "I'm sorry," I muttered, turning away. I'd only seen a dead body once before, and I'd never even been in a fight—at least not while sober. I couldn't believe I'd just killed my friend.

I fell away from Carl, and lay on my back in the dirt. I reached down and quickly wrenched the broken wooden stake from my leg, and felt myself get woozy. Gareth and Chelsea stood up, and the rest of the crowd followed suit, applauding my efforts loudly.

"Bravo to new recruit Reed in his debut fight," Gareth declared over the loudspeaker. "Just nine more to go and he can be a free man, and a rich one at that!"

"And I think my daughter Chelsea is a new fan," he joked, nudging her, causing her to blush. A moment later she looked down to catch eyes with me for a brief instant. His daughter? I couldn't believe it—I was relieved she wasn't his lover, but couldn't stomach that she was related to this monster.

I was nauseous as I glanced at Carl's body, just

feet away. I could still feel the sensation of the dagger slicing through his chest.

I felt dizzy, and as I stood up, my legs buckled underneath me. I sat down again and closed my eyes. My heart raced as I realized I was going to lose consciousness. The last thing I saw before the lights went out was the pool of my own blood beneath me.

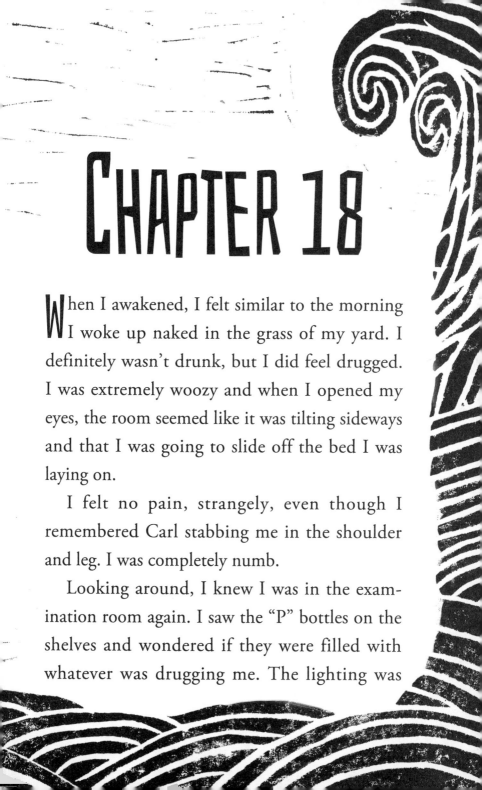

CHAPTER 18

When I awakened, I felt similar to the morning I woke up naked in the grass of my yard. I definitely wasn't drunk, but I did feel drugged. I was extremely woozy and when I opened my eyes, the room seemed like it was tilting sideways and that I was going to slide off the bed I was laying on.

I felt no pain, strangely, even though I remembered Carl stabbing me in the shoulder and leg. I was completely numb.

Looking around, I knew I was in the examination room again. I saw the "P" bottles on the shelves and wondered if they were filled with whatever was drugging me. The lighting was dim and I strained my head to scan the room on all sides. I was alone, but I could see that someone had applied bandages to my shoulder and leg.

"Let me out of here!" I yelled out, but no one responded. Despite feeling unsteady, I sat up and stumbled to the door. I reached out with my good arm, noticing for the first time the tug of an IV, and pulled on the handle as hard as I could. It didn't budge.

Before I could think twice about it, I grabbed the "P" bottles off the shelf and threw them violently to the ground. They shattered at my feet, sending stinky and sticky liquids and ointments splattering everywhere, and shards of glass across the floor.

Then, in a fit of exhaustion and my injuries throbbing, I collapsed back onto the bed and waited.

A few minutes later, I heard someone approaching and the door swung open after a series of beeps.

Elise strode in wearing a white lab coat and I saw her eyes run over my body, from top to bottom.

She stepped gingerly around the broken glass and came up to me, grabbing my arm and peered at me.

"You have to be careful, Reed," she said. "I heard you were an impressive fighter. Gareth's going to want to show you off some more, and soon."

"What does that mean?" I asked, feeling despondent.

"It means you have to conserve your energy," she said, nodding toward the broken glass at her feet. "Throwing a fit isn't going to get you anywhere, you know."

She reached over and started to pull away the layers of gauze at my shoulder that were soaked through with blood. She then reached into her pocket and pulled out another bottle, took off the cap, and swabbed the area, looking at me in the eye to see if I winced.

"The Praeclarus members loved you. I'm not

surprised, really. You fit the mold," she said as she wet a towel and squeezed it over my shoulder. The water dripped down and streaks of body paint and blood mixed together, falling to the floor in pools.

"What do you mean?" I asked. I couldn't tell if Elise was trying to help me or hurt me, but I wanted to glean as much information as possible from her if she was willing to share. My head was still foggy, but I sat up and looked her in the eye.

"Well, generally, Praeclarus likes the athletic, good-looking kids the best. Call it *schadenfreude*, or some perverse enjoyment of seeing half-naked teen-agers fight it out, I don't know . . . " she said as she continued to tend to my injuries. "The attractive ones become the fighters, and the rest become Suits."

"How long has this been going on?" I asked, since Elise was talking like these fights were a common occurrence.

"Too long, Reed," she said as she began to reapply a new gauze to me.

I was confused. Where did the other kids that fought come from? Why would people want to watch something like this?

"You have a lot of questions," Elise said, and I nodded. "Reed, they'll get answered in due time, I assure you. But you must lay low for a while. A small group of us are putting together a plan to escape," she spoke quietly and I wondered if anyone was listening in to us.

"Ames?" I asked.

She raised her eyebrows, but didn't say anything.

"And why are you telling *me* this?"

"We think you're the person we've been waiting for. The one who can help us," she said, grabbing my good arm's hand and squeezing it tightly.

"How? I don't understand—"

Just then, we heard footsteps coming down the hall and Elise hissed at me. "Whatever happens, you cannot say anything about this to anyone, you understand? If Gareth or anyone else gets wind of this, they'll kill us all," she said. "It's happened before. And I'll murder you myself if I think you're going to ruin this for us," she hissed.

Just as she said that, the door beeped and Ames walked in. He made eye contact with Elise.

"How's he doing? Gareth is asking," he said, coming over to look at the gauze over my shoulder wound.

"He's lucky. Just a few inches in a different direction and we'd be in trouble. He'll heal quickly, all things considered." Elise glanced at Ames, and they exchanged a worried look.

"Okay, I'll be sure to tell Gareth the good news," Ames said. He patted me on the other shoulder firmly. "I'll see you back in training soon, Reed. Now rest up, okay?"

"Sure," I said. I was exhausted and the drugs were making me want to go back to sleep. I closed my eyes and Elise sat next to me, resting her hand on my forearm.

As soon as I closed my eyes, my mind filled with the sight of Carl bleeding underneath me, reaching up to plead with me to help him. But I *couldn't* help him, just like my brother.

I twitched and tossed my body unhappily. I was starting to feel a burning sensation in my leg area. "Time for another dose, I take it," Elise said, and injected something into the IV in my arm.

Within minutes, I was sleepy again. When I woke up, it felt like hours later and my head was clear, but my shoulder and bad leg were throbbing. The IV had been removed.

"Ouch!" I yelled as I struggled to sit up.

"Here, let me help you," a familiar voice said, and I looked over. To my surprise, Chelsea was sitting next to me, her dark hair falling over her shoulders. She leaned over and her hair tickled my forearms as she reached around my back and helped to prop me up.

Even under the unflattering lighting of the room, she was perfect, and she smelled sweet and clean.

"What are you doing here?" I demanded,

remembering her sitting in the stands, watching me suffer. "What are you—some kind of monster? You cheered throughout my fight—I saw you!" I sputtered out, feeling the strain of my anger. My breathing was labored and I was exhausted.

"I wanted to make sure you're okay, Reed," she said, ignoring my angry words, smiling sweetly and looking at me with her big brown eyes. "You're sort of my pet project," she said.

"Your pet project? I'm nobody's pet project! What does that even mean?" I asked, feeling a hatred rise up in me.

"Just hear me out Reed, please," she said, as she reached over and rested her hand on my good leg. I felt a rush of electricity at her touch, and my face was burning up.

"Why would I listen to you? You watched me almost get killed . . . " I responded, confused about her intentions.

"Yes," Chelsea said.

"And, Gareth's your dad? I don't understand. How long have you been here?" I asked.

"Yes, he's my dad."

"So does that make you evil, too? Your performance out there sure made it seem like—"

"Reed!" she interrupted me. "I resent the accusation. I have no control over my dad and his horrible hobbies, but I have to play along."

"How can you watch someone die and not do anything?" I asked, feeling more ill as we talked, and I coughed hard, my whole head scratchy like it was stuffed with cotton balls. What kind of medicine had Elise given me?

"Reed, you need to take it easy and listen. My dad has vowed to put me away in solitary confinement if I don't act like the obedient daughter in front of all his buddies. Please! You have to believe me—"

I didn't say anything, feeling confused by what Chelsea was telling me. She continued to talk.

"I'm not supposed to be here you know, but

you're just so cute I wanted to see you again," she smiled at me and leaned in and gave me a kiss on the cheek.

Her hair tickled my skin and I couldn't help but recoil back.

"So, why are you here again?" I asked.

"If you ever want to get out of here alive, I can help you," she said, and she turned serious, staring at me with those hypnotic brown eyes, as if willing me to be on her side through her gaze alone.

"What do you mean? How?"

"Before I share anything more, you have to listen to me, and no one else, okay?" she said. I mumbled a yes and it felt like she was controlling my mind, as my resolve to doubt her intentions was softening. I didn't know what to think. Chelsea leaned over and hugged me and I tried not to wince from the pain of her putting weight against me.

"I'm working on a plan, but it's not ready yet," she said. "I promise you though, you want to be on my side."

And just like that, she was gone again. A little while longer, Elise walked in again, followed by two White Suits.

"Time to get transferred," she said, as she helped to lift me up by my good arm, and started to escort me out of the room. "There's nothing more I can do for you here in the treatment center."

The medicine she gave me made me woozy, but masked the pain of my injuries.

"Hopefully you won't be back any time soon," she said.

We walked through a maze of hallways until we got to a new room that I hadn't been to before. Elise opened the door and it appeared to be a small apartment.

There was a bed with a lamp next to it, a small kitchenette, an ugly leather couch, and an old-school TV on a stand.

"This is your new home for a bit, until you're better," Elise said as she escorted me in and led me to the couch.

"You'll take it easy here while you recuperate. I'll check in every day to see how you're feeling and to tend to your wounds," she said, looking back at the two White Suits that were standing right behind her.

"You need to rest up. You understand me?"

I nodded my head. "Okay," I said, and laid back on the sofa.

"What am I supposed to do here?" I asked, as she was leaving.

"Why don't you watch TV?" one of the White Suits suddenly chimed in. I was surprised to hear one of them talk.

Elise glared at him before slamming the door behind her, shutting me into the room.

I looked at the TV and sighed. It was very old, and I hadn't seen one like this—a flat box—except in movies. I knew that the door was locked, and taking stock of the room, there was nothing else to occupy my time.

I needed to find a way back to Micah, Delphine,

and the others to warn them what was happening. Next time one of the Suits came to deliver me food, I'd attack them and get out of here, I decided.

I waited for what felt like hours, and no one came. I was starving for my lunch and anxious for a Suit to walk into the room so I could try to escape.

As I was sitting there, I barely made out the sounds of distant cheers and wondered what was happening in the Coliseum.

Bored and anxious, I finally grabbed the remote control from next to the TV and turned it on.

My stomach dropped when I saw what was on the screen. At that moment, it was a close-up of Delphine, standing in the middle of the Coliseum floor.

She was wearing a white tank top and small shorts, and she was painted with long stripes of red, blue, and yellow over her tanned skin. If I hadn't known better, I might've thought she was a seasoned fighter, ready for whatever she faced.

But as the camera zoomed in, I thought I

recognized fear in her eyes as she looked around, taking in her surroundings.

There was a sudden cut to Gareth and he was addressing the people in the stands—"Isn't she remarkable?" he asked, and the crowd roared in approval. "She's shown a lot of promise in training, so I think you'll be pleased with this match-up," he said, and everyone quieted, anxious to hear who she'd be fighting.

There was a cut to the large metal gate as it lifted up, and the White Suits dragged Rose into the center of the ring. She kicked and screamed, like a pig being brought to slaughter.

"And then there's Rose," Gareth continued. "Sweet little Rose. She looks slight, but she's agile and I think there's a fighter in her. She just needs to prove herself. And if she doesn't, well, *c'est la vie*, right? Someone's gotta go," he joked and people laughed, the sounds echoing through my silent room.

Both Rose and Delphine held long swords and

I yelled at the TV, wishing there was anything I could do to halt what was about to happen.

The screen went back to a close-up of Delphine, who was beautiful in her warrior garb, her bright green eyes shining in HD. The fear on her face suddenly transformed to steely determination and I knew that Rose wasn't likely to make it out of this alive.

If Delphine survived this, I had to get her alone so I could share all that I knew about the island so far. If we were going to escape, we'd have to work together to make sense of the madness that surrounded us.